THE
ZING FLING

An Adventure in the Crystal Forest

Dee G Suberla

The Zing Fling
An Adventure in the Crystal Forest

Copyright © 2023 by Dee G. Suberla
Jacket and interior art copyright © 2023 by Philip Alera
All rights reserved.

Oak Line Press
518 S Rt 31
McHenry, IL 60050

Oak Line Press is a division of DG Suberla Consulting, LLC. The Oak Line Press name and logo are property of DG Suberla Consulting, LLC.

This book is a work of fiction. Names, characters, places, and incidents are the product of the author's imagination or are used fictitiously.

Any resemblance to actual events, locals, or persons, living or dead is coincidental.

ISBN: 979-8-9872703-1-8 (*paperback*)
       979-8-9872703-2-5 (*eBook*)
       979-8-9872703-3-2 (*Hardcover*)

Printed in the United States of America

Acknowledgements

There have been so many people over the years that have helped me with this book. First and foremost, Nan Hedden Mitchell and Carole L. White for insisting that I must have had a story somewhere that I could use so the three of us could go to the writers' club together. At that time, this was a one-page idea for a story.

Thank all of you for reading, commenting, listening, and brainstorming to help it move on: Toni Irwin, Jack Walsh, Lisa Walsh, Susan Lee, Lisa Farrugia Kym Vycital and Cindi Vycital. And again, Mom and Dad (Henrietta D. Vycital and Harold D. Vycital) for sitting through the first draft reading for three hours.

Thank you, Tiffany Harelik, for your support and guidance.

Table Of Contents

CHAPTER 1

The 18th King

Joey was sure that his bike rounded the corner of the driveway at the speed of light. His Polaroid camera flew almost straight-out sideways from the handlebars, pulling hard on the cord. At that instant, he stood on the pedals, jammed on the brakes, twisted his body, and leaned into the best skid of the day.

"Yeah!" he grunted, making his voice a little deeper. "Man, it must be a hundred degrees." He wiped the sweat off his face with the bottom of his favorite red T-shirt, the one with the Jamaican flag on it. He hopped off the bike and let it drop to the ground as his best friend Lou passed his house, having failed to match Joey's speed. "Ha! I won, Lou!"

Lou was Joey's best friend and lived five houses down from Joey, at 222 South Lake Drive in wonderful Kraspers

Lake in Northern Illinois. Lou yelled over his shoulder, "Later this week we have to visit the culvert — I've got a great story to tell you!"

"Ok Lou, I'll have one about how Crapper's Lake came to a full boil today!" Joey snickered to himself recalling how Lou came up with that one. They were seining for minnows last summer at the lake and tried using a torn bed sheet from Joey's old twin bed. They caught nothing. Lou was so frustrated that he blurted out "They should rename this toilet CRAPPER'S Lake, cuz that's all we're catching today — minnow crap."

Joey laughed so hard that day that he fell into the water. He enjoys spending time with Lou. Every now and then Joey would go with him to the culvert located a few blocks down. It ran under the main road leading to town. There was usually a trickle of water going through it, but it was built large enough for the cows to pass from one field to the other without having to cross the road. That was back in the day when most of this land was a giant cattle farm.

Joey was jolted from his daydream by his Stepdad who was a tad peeved, as usual. "Joseph Otto Rheelat! Get that bike in the garage now. A man's word is his bond, and you once again broke yours! You agreed to be on time and once again you're late! Get in here and clean yourself up! Now your mother and I will be late!"

"Okay, okay, I'm coming. And quit calling me Otto - I hate that!" He hollered right back at George. He muttered to himself as he stomped over to the garage door, "I hate it when he does that. Just because he's married to my mom doesn't give him the right to use that gross name. Geez!"

He bent over to fling the garage door open. That forced out an "Oooffff," because the garage door never flung open for him; he always had to muscle it. He heaved the heavy door up to his shoulders, pushed it straight up and spun around to grab the bike. Suddenly, his lips felt numb, and he was woozy. Just as his whole body began tingling, the world went black.

Joey was floating now, and it felt like he was bouncing back and forth, up and down. He didn't know where he was, but that was okay. It was cool and soothing, just like his waterbed. Something smelled sweet and familiar. And there were voices coming from somewhere … but he couldn't make out the words, and something was poking his butt. They were little pokes, like someone was poking him with a #2 pencil eraser. Still irritating, though.

"Mmmmm, must be a twitch," mumbled Joey.

"What? Oh George, he said something." His Mom sounded scared.

"Katie, what the heck did he say?" George was agitated.

"I don't know, something about a twitch."

"Oh, a twitch; ok then."

"Honey, open your eyes. It's Mom, Joey."

Joey opened his eyes to find his mother's nose three inches away from his. He was in his waterbed. "Are you okay, honey?" He recognized the smell of her perfume. She was wiping his forehead with a cool, damp cloth.

"Yeah, wha... what happened?"

George's voice came from behind his Mom's head, "You passed out kid. It's ninety-eight degrees out there and, by the looks of it, you were riding that bike pretty hard. It's called a heat stroke. You're a little young for that but it does happen to kids that don't think about taking it easy in this kind of heat. I'll leave you in your mother's capable hands now. I don't want to miss the game; Cubs just might make the finals this year!" Always full of concern, George was... for the Chicago Cubs that is.

His Mom fussed over him for a while, and finally left to get him a glass of water. Joey just laid there, clearing his head, trying to remember what had happened to him. He needed to figure out what was going on.

The one thing Joey did know was that he was in his comfy waterbed. This was one of his greatest finds in the deep end of the attack. It was his Dad's from years ago

when everyone was essentially sleeping on a bag of water encapsulated by a wood frame. The last thing he remembered was that he was getting yelled at by his step Dad by the garage and... *POKE!*

"What the heck *is* that?"

Something was poking his leg from inside the waterbed. He sat up fast but fell back faster.

"Ohhhh, I think I'm going to be sick."

He lay back down, his head — and the room — spinning a little too fast. Soon, he heard the clinking of ice in the hall just outside his room. Joey was glad when his Mom came back, but he knew better than to sit up.

"What did you say honey? Are you ok?" She was at his bedside. "Here's your water. Now just take little sips. George is calling the Carlsons to let them know we won't make it to the barbecue." Frank and Loretta Carlson were close friends with his Mom and George, as in they lived next door and they had known each other for as long as he could remember. Both George and Frank spent time in the military but Frank acts like a normal person where George acts like he's some kind of General or something. The two couples were always getting together to do boring things. The Carlsons had twin boys close to Joey's age and they were okay to hang out with. He could tolerate them long enough to enjoy their killer pool — it even had a diving board.

Joey sipped the cool water. He was relieved that he didn't get sick after all. It was nice that his Mom was so concerned, but it seemed like an hour before she decided he wasn't going to die and left him alone so he could sleep. He was exhausted. Before she left, she lifted the picture from his dresser and said, "You really captured that deer, Joey. You are going to be a great photographer someday." He had felt proud the first million times she said that, but now Joey just rolled his eyes. She finally set it back down next to the picture of his Dad and left the room.

He wouldn't admit it to his mom but that picture was one of his favorites, too. It was a picture of a big buck standing at the edge of the woods behind the house. He took that one with his digital camera, but he still loved his old Polaroid. There was something awesome about the racket it made while spitting out the picture. It still had two pictures left in the cartridge. The clunky old camera was stored near the waterbed up in the attic, it belonged to his Dad and Joey loved it. He created a small album of about ten Polaroids, great shots where he captured somebody laughing hysterically, mouth open — all teeth and throat. Just thinking about it made him smile as he drifted off to sleep.

When he woke up it was almost dark. He was hungry and had to go to the bathroom, really bad, but he was afraid to sit up. After a little while he was more afraid of wetting the bed than sitting up, so he moved slowly, swaying along with the movement of the waterbed. When Joey stood up, he took a quick inventory - he felt weak but otherwise okay. He blushed as he pulled his gym shorts over his underwear. His Mom and George must have undressed him when they put him in bed. He shook his head all the way to the bathroom.

Just after he shut the door he heard a soft *knock, knock, knock*. "Joey, are you in there?"

"No Mom, it's a two-headed alien from Alpha Centauri!" He hated it when she talked to him through the bathroom door.

"Well, Mr. Smart Mouth Alpha Centaurian guy, there's a sandwich in Joey's room. I hope your people like bologna. Don't forget to wash your hands or tentacles or whatever it is that you use to pick up food. And turn out the bathroom light when you're done." He heard her giggling a bit as she went back down the stairs.

Back in his bedroom, he stood in front of his dresser mirror and inspected his thirteen-year-old frame. He looked a little pale and too skinny, as usual.

"What a dork! You can't even ride your bike without messing up and giving George more material to taunt you with for the next hundred years."

He sneered at himself, shook his head and turned his attention to the sandwich and glass of pop on the nightstand. While eating, he contemplated the ever-swirling debate around "pop" vs. "soda." Pop - soda, whatever! Who cares? Debate over.

After he finished eating, he crawled back into bed and started drifting off to sleep when… *POKE, POKE, POKE!*

"Now it's on my foot. What the heck is that?" He threw the covers off the waterbed, knelt by the foot of the bed, and slipped the sheet up. He saw the tiniest movement near the water mattress cap. He leaned over and laid his ear on the cool vinyl. *Whir, wisp, click, gurgle, whirrr...*

He snapped his head up. "What the heck?"

His eyes bulged and his heart raced. He whispered, "Oh great, now I'm crazy. Just freakin' awesome!"

He saw the movement again. "Okay, that's it." Joey unscrewed the cover to the cap, looped his index finger into the loop on the cap and pulled it out. He carefully leaned down again to listen again without disturbing the water.

Gurgle, glip, glop, whirrr...

The noises were louder now. As he leaned over to look in, a blast of warm air threw him back. Then came a loud swish and a *ZINNNG!*

In the next second, a four-foot diameter, multi-colored transparent ball hovered over his bed. It hung there for a moment… then *ZINNNG,* it burst wide open! The room was a kaleidoscope. There were colors everywhere: green, silver, orange, red, blue and a hundred other shades. There were sparkles and squiggles that tickled as they fell on him. In the back of his mind, he thought he should be afraid, but he was amazed.

POP! ZING! FWAPP! A short man appeared on the bedroom floor. He rolled around giggling and rubbing his belly. And as if that wasn't enough, Joey heard wind chimes.

"Hello Joey, my boy! I'm Wheedles of Waiderfled, the Eighteenth King of the Zing Fling. This is so, because in fact, I have successfully completed my very first Zing Fling!"

The little man jumped up and stood with his stubby legs spread apart. He was no taller than Joey's chest and held a crooked purple stick above his head as high as he could. He wore a rumpled yellow tunic over a bright green shirt and baggy orange pants. There was a leather pouch over one shoulder and a wide leather belt around his chubby waist. But the wildest thing of all were all the colored balls floating around his long, light blue hair. He was still laughing, and he just sort of ... twinkled.

"By the look on that face of yours, I can tell that you have never been involved with a Zing Fling before. Well, Joey my boy, it is the way I travel to wherever I'm needed."

CHAPTER 2

What's a Ho-dree?

"Look, Mr. Waddles or whoever you are. You've got a lot of nerve crashing into my bedroom like this." Joey stood with his arms crossed, trying to look tough while the sparkles and squiggles continued to tickle him.

With that, the chimes stopped, and this Waddles guy looked like he was going to cry. Suddenly, there was a *CRACK!* and one of the colored balls, an orange one, shattered. The pieces turned into a gray dust and disappeared into the brown carpet.

"My name is Wheedles, and I must have made a mistake," Wheedles said softly. He sat down and laid his purple stick across his lap. "You were supposed to be a special young man who needed me, not a boy who would shatter my dreams." Wheedles looked so sad and beaten that Joey felt terrible.

He realized that he had just become George for a minute and now he was ashamed of himself.

"I'm so sorry, Wheedles — it's just that you scared the heck out of me. Look, I've had a pretty bad day and I'm kind of confused right now. I didn't mean to shatter your dreams or anything." As Joey spoke, he walked over and knelt by Wheedles. Getting this close he could see two more things. First off, this little guy's skin seemed iridescent, like mother-of-pearl, only super soft. The second thing was his tears. They were so transparent he could hardly see them, but they were there, and Joey had caused them. He didn't know what was happening, but he was certain there was a lot more going on than he could even imagine right now.

He laid his hand on Wheedles' shoulder, "I don't know if I need you or not. Man, I don't even know if you're real. But, hey, it would be an honor to have a friend like you."

Wheedles looked up at him with rainbow eyes and smiled. A new ball appeared between them and after a second, it split in two, creating a silver one and an orange one. "I'm sorry if I scared the heck out of you Joey, I would be honored to help you find your heck and put it back in."

The silver ball followed Joey as he leaned back, away from Wheedles. The orange one joined the rest of the balls over Wheedles' head.

"That's ok Wheedles, my heck is just fine where it is, wherever it is." Joey remained focused on the silver ball.

As Wheedles jumped up he hollered, "Well, bless my soul by the winds and sea, you are my friend and you do need me! Joey, you already made your first ho-dree without even trying."

Joey was leaning backward with his knees up and his arms stretched out behind him. He was looking cross-eyed at the silver ball floating right in front of him. "Ho-dree? Is that what this thing is? Why is it following me?"

"Joooeeey," his Mom called from the stairs.

"Uh, yeah Mom?" Joey's ho-dree was mesmerizing.

"Are you okay up there? Are you playing music?"

"Uh, yeah Mom."

"Well turn it down. It is 9:30 and you should try to get more rest."

"Okay."

Wheedles bunched his shoulders up and giggled. "Mom? Is that what you call your Mimi?"

"What's a Mimi?"

"That's who helps the Da-Wonn!"

"What's a Da-Wonn? No, don't tell me, it's the Dad, right?"

"Well, my friend, I can see we both have much to teach. Let's get down to work."

Wheedles closed the bedroom door. He waved the purple stick in front of the door and chanted,

> "A threshold you are,
>
> now magic you'll be,
>
> let Mimi see,
>
> what she needs to see."

He made more of those *whir-click-gurgle* noises. As he did this, transparent purple waves flowed out of the stick and covered the door. Wheedles kept on *gurgling* and *whirring* and started turning in circles faster and faster until he was spinning, and he somehow floated up to the middle of the door.

Joey heard a *ZING* and a *SNAP* and Wheedles was back on the floor and the door looked perfectly normal again.

"What was that all about?" Joey was sitting cross-legged and forgot about the ho-dree floating above his head as he slipped on the T-shirt that was lying on the floor next to him.

"That's so your Mimi won't worry. See?" And right on queue there were three little knocks and the door slowly opened; Joey's Mom came in. She went to his bed acting like she was pulling the covers up, over him as though he was there sleeping. But he was not. Joey was sitting on the floor by the closet.

"Mom, what are you doing?" She ignored him and tip-toed away from the bed. She turned off the light and closed the door behind her. But the room was still light, bright with colors and squigglies and sparkles and ho-drees.

Wheedles was dancing in circles in front of Joey, waving his wand and chanting in those noises again. After he started spinning, Joey heard,

> "Special boy come with me,
> you'll be amazed at what you see,
> don't be afraid for safe you'll be,
> with the Eighteenth King of the Zing Fling."

Joey jumped up, grabbed his Polaroid, and *WHOOSH - ZIIINNNNGGGG*. He dropped it just as they were both whisked out of his room… house… or possibly out of this world.

"OOOHHHH NOOOO!" Joey sounded like he was yodeling and under normal circumstances he would have been embarrassed but now he was trying to hold on to his senses. He was on a roller coaster up, up, up, down, down, down. Colors were everywhere around him. He could feel them touching him; he breathed them in and out. They formed a funnel that he and Wheedles traveled through. This was one sick roller coaster. Although he couldn't hear him, he could see Wheedles was laughing and really enjoying the ride. Joey's stomach flip-flopped as he twirled and spun, head over heels, left to right, up and down — no wait - he was flying!

Then, *WHAM!* He hit the ground and rolled down a small hill. He stopped flat on his back and saw ... saw what, the sky? It was just like Wheedles' eyes, all rainbows.

"Oh man, Lou is never going to believe this!"

CHAPTER 3

Welcome to Waiderfled

"Joey?" Wheedles stood over him leaning on his purple wooden stick. "Joey, my friend, stand up and look around. I welcome you to Waiderfled!" Wheedles bowed in Joey's direction.

Joey's ho-dree followed him as he rolled over and sat up. This was a sight that was beyond anything he could have ever imagined. People (if that's what they were — Joey wasn't sure) like Wheedles stood around clapping and talking in their *click-whir-gurgle* language. They were all unusual colors and shades. Both young and old had wilder hairstyles than any 1980s punk rocker and, of course, floating above each crazy-colored head was at least one ho-dree, and some had four or more.

On the ground, several types of furry little animals scurried about; some had two legs, some had four, and some had six. They made vowel sounds like "*eeeeee oooooo yeeeuuu*". They didn't have ho-drees, but over their heads they did have something that reminded Joey of the fizzies he felt tickle his nose when he sipped from a full glass of pop or soda or whatever.

As he looked around Joey asked, "Wheedles, what is going on? Is this a carnival?"

"Well, I don't know what a carn-val is…"

"Carn-a-val," Joey interrupted.

Wheedles continued, "I don't know what that is, but this is a welcome reception for us both. You are my first Zing Fling and the town is excited to have a new Zing Fling King in place again. It has been a long time."

By now Joey was back to looking around. He'd have to know more about what this Zing Fling thing is all about, but for now — WOW. The buildings were spectacular; some sported purple and green checkerboard, some were covered in yellow and pink stripes. They were big and round, small and square, long and triangular. There were babies in backpacks and kids with one-wheeled contraptions that had big cushy seat pillows. Two sticks came up on either side of the wheel and great big wings flared out from behind the seat. Joey looked up and saw a girl riding one. To be more accurate, she was *flying* one. Her hands pushed then pulled the sticks and the big wings moved up and down gracefully while the wheel spun.

She looked down at him and smiled. She let go of a stick long enough to wave and flick her pink hair behind her shoulder. Then quick as a blink, she grabbed a pink ho-dree from above her head and tossed it down to him.

Wheedles looked up at her and said, "Good day, Lita. My friend thanks you for your gift."

Joey caught the ho-dree from where he sat; it was smoother and heavier than he expected. He turned to say something to Wheedles, but Lita caught his eye again. He watched her fly into the bizarre forest behind them and wondered what it would be like just to stand next to her and have a conversation. But honestly, he didn't think he'd be able to speak while standing so close to that beautiful creature. And Joey was sure she was a magical creature of some sort and what the heck do you say to them? She *glistened*. As he watched her fly off he felt his heart banging into his chest wall and the roughness of his jeans as he dried off his sweaty palms.

As Lita flew into the trees, Joey saw that they were enormous and see-through, with brown and green veins running through them. Even the leaves were transparent. When the breeze blew, it sounded like music from a thousand strings like harps, guitars, and violins, like the background music when you entered heaven. Yeah, maybe he *was* in heaven, maybe the heat stroke was a stroke-stroke that killed him…but everything was just fine — so much to see!

There were large insects flying around inside the forest. Joey guessed they were large dragonflies or maybe hummingbirds with dragonfly-like wings. They darted in and out and sparkled when the sunlight caught their wings. He wanted to get closer and catch one. Oh, how he wished he had brought his Polaroid camera!

It was all too much. Joey was so taken with everything; he had to lay back down. It was then that Joey realized that Wheedles was standing over him smiling. Once he had Joey's attention he asked, "What do you think?"

"It is amazing, magical, beautiful — I don't know … I just can't believe it."

Suddenly, the crowd stopped clapping, babies started crying and the animals began whining. He looked at Wheedles, who was now frowning. Joey was about to say something else when he noticed his silver ho-dree turning midnight blue. In that instant the ho-dree dropped down and bonked him right on the forehead. For the second time that day, Joey was out like a light.

He opened his eyes and looked around his own bedroom. He was on the floor near the closet when his Mom opened the bedroom door.

"What on Earth are you doing on the floor and why is your bed all torn apart? Good heavens, you took the cap off the bed. What is the matter with you Joey? Do you realize what kind of mess this could have made?" She picked the cap up off the floor.

"Wait Mom, don't."

"What? What do you mean '*don't*'? You mean don't put the cap back on so that you can jump on the bed and flood the living room downstairs? I don't know why on Earth I let you keep this silly waterbed. Nobody sleeps in waterbeds anymore, most people your age don't even know what they are! We need to get serious about buying you a real bed. I wanted you to have one of those bunkbed setups with the desk underneath but no, you had to have your Dad's waterbed. Well, if this thing overflows, or worse, breaks, it's going to cost a fortune to fix. You can't take this cap off the mattress. As a matter of fact, I'm going to have to agree with George on this one, let's start looking for a new bedroom set as soon as possible. I'm done with this waterbed nonsense — what was I thinking?"

She tossed the cap on the bed and spoke over her shoulder as she left the room, "Get showered and dressed and come downstairs. Breakfast is almost ready."

Joey felt a little stiff and it took him a minute to clear his head. "Wow, what a dream." He brought his hands up to rub his face and felt something in his hand. He opened his right hand and there was a small rock. It looked like a rose quartz crystal, all pink with cracks running through it. He gazed at it for a moment and then spoke out loud without even realizing it, "OMG, is this Lita's ho-dree? Um. I guess it wasn't a dream."

He sat up and quickly ducked his head and looked around for his silver (and now, midnight blue) ho-dree. "Good, it's gone!" He jumped up from the floor and opened the junk drawer in his dresser. He pulled out an old gray box from one of George's tie pins and slid the quartz ho-dree into it. Then Joey set the box on the dresser next to the pictures of the deer in the woods and his Dad.

C H A P T E R 4

Banished From Waiderfled

"George, have you noticed anything different about Joey?"

"You know…since he passed out the day before yesterday, he does seem a little distant. It's like he sort of slowed down or something; he's a mystery to me." George spoke while he loaded the dinner dishes into the dishwasher. "I just can't figure that kid out. I lose my patience with him. He is so… I don't know… detached. His brain is not fully attached to his body, and he has no self-discipline. Okay, he's just chronically distracted, and clumsy. I guess he could grow out of it, but I seriously doubt it."

"Or maybe he's just twelve, George. As far as that goes, I don't think it's chronic." Joey's Mom's tone cut the air as she looked out the kitchen window. "Did you know he slept on

22

the floor? He doesn't seem to want to sleep in his waterbed …and he's so quiet. I'm worried."

"Well, that's a mother's job, I guess. Have you tried talking to him?" George walked over to the table, picked up his glass and gulped down the last of his iced tea.

At that moment, Joey bounded down the stairs, clutching the pink rock in his hand. In classic Joey fashion, he was looking at it as he ran and sure enough, he felt the toe of his shoe grab onto the carpet and *WHAM!* — he was on the floor at the bottom of the stairs. The rock went flying, hit the front door, then fell to the floor.

"Joey! What happened?" his Mom yelled as she came around the corner.

"I'm okay Mom, don't worry. I tripped."

"Of course, you did. Did ya hurt the floor?" The smirk on George's face was irritating.

"Ha, ha George, very funny." Joey's frustration showed in his voice and on his face.

"I'm just kidding but Joey, you should really be more careful. You need to learn to focus. You are always so dang distracted!" George was actually looking at Joey's Mom with one eyebrow raised as if to say — "You see what I mean?"

By now Joey was up and retrieving his rock. "I guess I wasn't paying attention. I'm going outside for a while."

"Did you want to help your Mom clean the oven first?" George chuckled the same way he always did when he made fun of Joey. Teasing Joey was George's favorite pastime. It seemed like all he ever did, but Joey suspected that his Stepdad had more to say to him, but never quite did… he hinted at it through teasing. *Not interested, George,* Joey thought *and right now your opinion of me is obvious.*

"Real funny, George — could you just quit talking about that?!"

"You're a bright kid, Joey, but sometimes I swear you act as dumb as a box of rocks." George was laughing, but slightly less creepily than usual. Very slightly.

"George, leave him alone, he was only trying to help. Now stop it." Joey's Mom was trying to scold George, but it was obvious she thought it was funny too. Joey let the screen door slam shut on his way out.

Joey thought back to that day for about the millionth time. It was almost three weeks ago when his Mom went to the store, and Joey thought he'd help her out by cleaning the oven. She had been complaining that she needed to get that done but there just wasn't any time. And he'd watched her do it before a bunch of times; how hard could it be? Get some gloves, spray the inside and wait. At least he could get it started for her and do the oven door. He sprayed the cleaner on the inside of the oven door and some of it splashed onto the floor. When he wiped it up, he noticed that the floor was shiny clean.

So, Joey decided that a super clean floor would be an added bonus for his Mom! He sprayed the oven cleaner over a big section of the floor and started wiping away while he waited the thirty minutes for the oven door to come clean.

By the time he was halfway through with the section of the floor he'd sprayed, he noticed that the oven cleaner seemed to be eating the vinyl floor. He tried to work faster, pushing himself until his shoulder, elbow and knees were all throbbing — but it was too late. Almost a third of the kitchen floor was ruined.

When his Mom got back from the store, she found Joey sitting in the middle of the ruined floor. "I'm s-s-sorry Mom. I thought I'd surprise you an... an..." he croaked. But he lost the battle to the huge lump in his throat, and the tears burning his eyes, and he dissolved into cry-baby sobs.

At first Joey's Mom was fuming, but as Joey got the story out in bits and pieces, she calmed down and let him finish. She even laughed a little trying to make Joey feel better, but he felt sooooo stupid!

Joey jerked himself back to reality — or whatever he was in these days — as he ran through the grass. *Well, now I know what humiliation is.* He just wanted to forget the whole horrible incident — he shook his head and made his way to the backyard.

Joey was laying back, looking up at the clear blue sky. He let his mind drift back to the rainbow sky in Waiderfled (which was certainly a much better memory than the stupid oven fiasco). He was wondering what it would be like to live someplace with a sky like that when he heard the *flip-flop* of his Mom's sandals coming towards him through the grass.

"Joey? Joey, what are you doing?"

"Nothing, Mom." Joey knew by the sound of her voice that she was in a mood to talk.

"You know, you've been awfully quiet lately. Something on your mind, kiddo?"

"I don't know, why?"

"Because you haven't been yourself, and that worries me. If there's something going on with you, sweetheart, I'd really like to know about it. I know I'm just your Mom and all, but I might even be able to help."

Joey knew he needed to come up with something or she'd never let him rest.

"Oh, Mom, I don't know. Sometimes it just bugs me that no matter what I do, I mess things up."

"What do you mean honey?"

"Well, every time I clean my room, you clean it after me. And George won't let me forget how I messed up the wax job on his car last June. How was I supposed to know you don't smear the wax all over the whole car before you start to wipe it off? No one told me to do a little bit at a time! And he keeps rubbing it in over the whole kitchen floor thing. I can't even ride my bike without passing out like a little baby." Joey figured this explanation would do for now. No way was he going to tell her what was really on his mind.

"Joey, passing out is not being a baby. What you had was heat exhaustion. It's perfectly normal — grown-ups pass out, too, you know. And George isn't trying to remind you about the wax job and the kitchen floor, he's just teasing you, he thinks he's funny. You know that. He cares a lot about you. George never had any of his own kids and he thinks teasing you is a good way to bond — he just doesn't get it sometimes. But he does love you, and he wants the very best for you. Of course, the fact that he was a sergeant in the Army taught him a lot. He values what he learned and tries to share that with you but it doesn't really come across as a sign of affection. Just know he means well."

"And you really had me going until you mentioned cleaning your room. Confidentially, I don't recall the last time you cleaned your room!" She smiled and nudged Joey with her elbow. "And I'm not really sure exactly what you're talking about here, Mister, but let me remind you that Mr. Framisnky says you do great work cleaning up the glass shop.

He said you're even getting pretty good at fixing screens and wood framed windows. He says you've got the same talent he saw in your Dad when he worked there. That's why he took the time to make you that piece of two-way mirror you're always carrying around in your pocket."

Joey had forgotten about his lucky two-way mirror now that he had Lita's ho-dree. Somehow, he felt a little closer to his Dad when he had the mirror with him, even though he had never even met his Dad. Joey knew that he worked at the glass shop for a while and, in a way, there was a connection to him there. That's why he liked the two-way mirror; it was easy to imagine his Dad could see him through it, even though Joey couldn't see his Dad. He figured that this might be close to how heaven worked.

"Joey, are you listening?"

"Yeah, Mom, great — my one claim to fame is sweeping! Big deal!"

"Not just sweeping honey, screens and windows, too. Don't you like your job?"

"Yeah, I like it, even though it's only every other Saturday. But c'mon Mom, it's not like I'm performing brain surgery. You make it sound like it means something."

"Well, it does, Mr. I-*Can't*-Do-Anything-Right. It doesn't matter what you're doing, you'd better do your best. And… don't belittle yourself like that. It is just plain wrong to focus on the things that you don't do well, then completely dismiss those things you do well. It's just not playing fair. You are not the judge of what is valuable to people in this life, your job is to just do the very best job you can with anything you do. When things go wrong, pay attention — learn — do better next time. That's your real job right now, learn. It's not just pushing a broom, it's showing up, being kind, being thorough and being someone Mr. Framinsky can depend on. And here is where I completely agree with George: Do your job and do it well! Honey, really, is this what's wrong?"

"Yeah, Mom, that's it." This was getting out of control. Joey shifted into distraction mode. "Hey. Mom, is there any ice cream left?"

"Sure, rainbow sherbet — want some?"

"*Rainbow*…? No, never mind. I'm going to go listen to some music. Mom, do you know what a ho-dree is?"

"A ho- what?"

"A ho-dree."

"No, I can't say that I do. Is that what you're calling your two-way mirror now?"

"Yeah." Joey just shook his head.

She smiled and reached her hand down toward him. He took it and let her help him up. She let go of his hand and he felt the pressure of her grasp on his shoulder as she ruffled his thick brown hair with the other and said, "I love you, Joey — you know that, don't you?"

Joey rolled his eyes again, "Yeah, Mom, I know." Joey checked his jeans pocket; Lita's ho-dree was still there.

He went up to his bedroom and closed the door. He just stood there a minute and looked at his waterbed. "Wheedles, where are you? What did I do wrong?"

He walked to his nightstand appreciating the thick carpet cradling each step with his bare feet. As he picked up the small two-way mirror he spoke to it, "There you are!"

It was dark brown with polished edges. The idea of a mirror that you could see through on one side fascinated him. He made a game out of finding two-way mirrors in the local stores. They were easy to spot because of the color. Two-way mirrors have a different tint than regular mirrors, a little darker and slightly brownish. Mr. Carlson showed Joey the trick by comparing a normal piece of mirror to the two-way mirror and it became obvious. There was one in the wall behind the service desk at Etta & Cleo's Grocery in town. The gas station on the corner had one too, behind the cashier. Sometimes the place where the mirror is located gives it away. Other times, when he wondered if it was a two-way mirror or not, he would either do the fingernail test or the knocking test. Mr. Framinsky explained these techniques. "Okay Joey, the fingernail test is done by touching the glass with your fingernail. If the reflection has a little space between your nail and the reflection, it's a regular mirror. If the fingernail and reflection are touching, it's a two-way. Of course, if you have any doubts, just knock on the mirror. It should sound solid - like there's a wall behind it. If it sounds hollow, there are eyes, or even a camera behind it. Just remember that tint, touching nails, and hollow sound equals a two-way mirror. Be on your best behavior."

Joey held the two-way mirror in front of his dresser mirror and tilted it just a little. This is what he figured infinity was. He looked at himself in the dresser mirror and checked the area above his head for the millionth time. "Was it really just a dream?"

He pulled out Lita's ho-dree to look at it again and went over to the bed. He slid the ho-dree into the front pocket of his jeans and tucked the mirror in his shirt pocket and buttoned the flap. He made sure the water mattress cap was on tight and flopped on the bed and let the waves rock him. "And that folks, is why I love my waterbed — it's all about the rocking waves." He tried to empty his mind by thinking about infinity. After ten minutes or so, he fell asleep.

POKE! POKE! POKE!

Chapter 5

The Worst Word in Waiderfled

Joey's eyes popped open, and he lay there on his side, staring straight ahead. His nose was bent up just a little from the pillow and the mirror weighed heavy in his shirt pocket. *POKE, POKE, POKE.* "Yep, that's it, right on the side of my knee!" He jumped off the bed, flung the covers back, unscrewed the cover, and pulled the cap out. He sat back and waited. He was so excited; it was hard to breathe. He looked from the hole in the mattress to the area above the bed and back again. He heard a *BLINK* behind him. He turned and saw Wheedles standing in the shadows by the closet.

"Wheedles, you came back. What happened?" As Joey stood up, he saw that Wheedles looked mad. Really mad.

"*What happened?*" Wheedles mimicked Joey and raised a bushy blue eyebrow so high it disappeared under his bangs. "*What happened* was the same thing that *always* happens whenever someone says that word. Do you have *any idea* how many people you hurt?"

"How did I hurt people? I didn't do anything, and I didn't say anything bad. What are you talking about, Wheedles?"

"You don't know? You *really* don't know?" Wheedles seemed surprised.

Joey shook his head slowly. "Know what? What happened?"

Wheedles stepped out of the shadows and looked at Joey. "Sit down my friend, there's teaching to be done. You see, when you said the nasty word ..."

"What nasty word?" Joey remained standing.

"What — do you want me to say it now?"

"Say it, spell it, act it out, whatever! I don't remember saying anything. All I remember is a weird town, with strange people, a girl named Lita who threw me a ho-dree and that wild forest. Then I laid down and ..."

"Stop right now! Don't say it again!"

"Say *what* again?" Joey was frustrated.

"Calm down. Let me explain. You said that you… uh… you… er… you were *unable to believe* what was happening. Except, you used the bad word, the worst word, the hurt word." Wheedles was trying hard, but Joey was even more confused after the explanation than before it. "Okay, Joey. If you would have said `I <u>can</u> believe this,' we'd be up to our eyeballs in Waiderfled fun, but you said something else. You said the nasty word; it's the language of the enemy within. You must promise never to say it again."

"Wheedles, I <u>can'</u>... oops, I mean, it will be very hard to promise that. Please understand, it's not a bad word where I come from. People say it all the time. Why is it considered so bad in Waiderfled?" Joey sat down on the floor.

"Do you remember what happened after you said it?"

"Well, people quit laughing, you got mad, babies cried, and… oh yeah… my ho-dree turned dark blue and attacked me."

"Pretty good recall, my friend. That was quite a bonk on the noggin'." Wheedles stopped pacing, leaned on his purple stick, and looked directly into Joey's chocolate eyes.

"Your ho-dree did not attack you, you almost broke it. When you used that word, you really meant you *would not* believe what you were doing and seeing. It was not that you were *unable* to believe; it was that you *decided* not to believe. When you choose not to believe, you have no hope, no dream of believing. And that's what ho-drees are Joey — they are hopes and dreams. By saying what you said, you let the enemy within suck the life out of your ho-dree as well as the one Lita shared with you. Yours is lying back there in the grass, a dark blue rock; we couldn't find Lita's. And that's really a shame because only very special Waderfladens can share their ho-drees with others, and that Lita is one special Waderfladen!

As Joey leaned back and reached into the pocket of his jeans, he concluded on his own that a Waderfladen is a being from Waiderfled. He held the rose quartz ho-dree out in front of Wheedles. "I thought Waiderfled was a dream until I found this."

"By the rivers that run and the powers that be, you kept Lita's ho-dree, so you must believe! You *are* a special someone, this is certain. We have to get back to Waiderfled at once. We'll go see Mimi-Uno; she'll help us breathe life back into both ho-drees. Then we can get down to business."

"You know Wheedles, I get the feeling you've got some kind of plan here that involves me, but I don't have a clue as to what it is." Joey stood up and put his hands on his hips. "And what's this enemy stuff?"

Wheedles ignored him and went ahead with the threshold magic force-field. Joey realized what was happening and made a beeline for his Polaroid. He just grabbed the strap and - *WHOOSH* - he was on the Zing Fling roller coaster again.

Soaring up and down, over and over, covered in colors inside and out, Joey heard his own voice trailing off behind him, "Here we go again!"

Chapter 6

Return to Waiderfled

He hit the ground on his butt this time, cradling the camera in his lap. "Man, Wheedles, do we have to hit so hard?"

"Sorry, Joey — I'm still trying to get the hang of this. I'll try to do better next time."

"Next time?"

"Oh yes, next time! I am the Eighteenth King of the Zing Fling, and I'll be doing this for the rest of my life. It's my *zwarry*."

"*Zwarry*? What's that?"

"*Zwarry*, you know, my life plan."

"I think that's called 'destiny' where I come from." Joey looked around. "Is it night time now?" It wasn't completely dark, more like dusk or twilight.

"Yes Joey, it's very late and everyone is sleeping. They're still trying to get over your... ah... shall we call it your performance from more than a week ago? Let's go to my house and prepare for our journey."

"More than a week? That happened the day before yesterday. Waiderfled sure has short days!"

"They're not short; they last a whole day! What have you got there, Joey?" Wheedles was looking at the camera.

"Oh, it's my camera, want me to take your picture?" Joey pulled the camera up into position.

"No, don't do it. What is that thing?" Wheedles looked scared.

"It's just an old Polaroid camera, Wheedles — it won't hurt you."

"It looks wrong to me. Please don't take my, whatever that is. I'd just as soon hold on to my whatever it is... thank you. I think." Wheedles bent over and picked something up. "Here, Joey, I think this is yours." He tossed it to Joey, and it hit the camera.

Joey lowered the camera and felt around on the grass and found a midnight blue rock. "My ho-dree?"

"Yep, try not to lose it again before we see Mimi-Uno. Get yourself up and let's get going. There is much to do to prepare for our journey." Wheedles turned toward town.

As Joey got up, he noticed the night sky for the first time. "Geez, it doesn't look real!"

"What doesn't look real?"

"The sky. Look at it Wheedles — the stars are so big and there are so many unusual colors. And look! They keep changing! It looks like a cartoon sky!"

Wheedles looked up indifferently. He shrugged his shoulders and raised a bushy blue eyebrow. "What's a katoon sky?"

"*Cartoon!* Never mind, let's go."

They both shrugged it off and made their way around the edge of the strange-looking town. They stopped at a turquoise and white diagonally striped building and went to the front door. On the walls of the house there was either an orange circle or a purple star, every foot or so in all directions. The house itself had two shapes; it looked like a box sitting in front of a big ball. Joey thought it looked a little ridiculous, but he said, "Nice house. Is it yours?"

"It belongs to all of Waiderfled; it is the home of the Zing Fling King. I have been here for just over a week now."

When they reached the front step, Wheedles got down on one knee, and laid his purple stick across his lap. He began speaking solemnly in the *whir-gurgle* language again, which really didn't sound very solemn at all, and every now and then, Joey thought he heard a word he could understand.

"*Whir*... honor ... *gurgle* ... kings." Wheedles spoke for more than a minute.

While this was going on, a little pink animal approached and rubbed Joey's ankle like a cat, except this was no cat. It looked like a big pink ant with six legs and a corkscrew tail with a white tuft of hair at the end. Its pink and white-checkered eyes were shaped like great big cat eyes. The hair on its face was white, too, with long, thick, pink whiskers. The body was covered in white fur with pink spots. Joey thought he could hear the pink fizzies above its head. The scalloped ears seemed too big for its head. They reminded him of the flower petals little kids draw, all loopy. He guessed the little ant-cat was purring because it was making a thick, gravelly *"ee-uuuuuuuu"* sound in its throat.

Wheedles stood up and smiled at Joey and the ant-cat. He raised his hand behind his head, bowed, and brought his hand back around to his face. As he straightened up, he extended his arm toward the ant-cat.

"*Gurgle, garp,* welcome, *whir.*"

"EE-uuuuuuuu," it purred.

They both looked at Joey. Taking his cue, Joey did the same bowing ritual that Wheedles did, and when he extended his arm to both of them, he said, "Toooo youuuuuuuuu tooooo." That appeared to confuse them a little, but nobody said anything. Wheedles opened the door and they all went in.

CHAPTER 7

Lita and the Crystal Forest

The house lit up as they walked in. The light was shimmering, like light reflecting off water. It reminded Joey of the time the Carlson twins, Derrick and Donald, invited him over to swim in their pool at night. There was a full moon, and they had those solar lights all over the place making things a bit shimmery. It was almost mystical and then George started in with a ton of stupid Dad jokes, completely entertaining himself and disregarding all of the groans and eye-rolls from everyone else. So humiliating! How could he not know that he was the only one laughing?!!! Definitely not the only time he failed to read the room.

The inside of the house was simple. Joey couldn't help but think about what Lou would say right now. They entered through the small foyer with a large over-filled bookshelf,

42

then passed through to the small kitchen where there was a huge wooden table in the middle of the room. It looked old, but sturdy. There was a soft humming sound that Joey couldn't place but it added another dimension to the environment that was simply relaxing. Wheedles took the leather pouch off his shoulder and set it on the table. On his way to the bedroom, he set his purple stick in the corner of the kitchen.

While Wheedles was busy, Joey pulled the Polaroid camera from its case to check how many pictures he had left. "Darn, only two." He figured he'd better save them. There were going to be a gazillion things he'd want pictures of, especially Lita. He had to be very selective. He set his camera down next to Wheedles' pouch. The ant-cat was still hanging around Joey's feet and purring.

Wheedles came back into the kitchen. "I'm going to prepare our supplies for the journey. You two better get some rest." Wheedles opened a cabinet.

"You two? Is this thing coming with us?" Joey pointed to the ant-cat.

"Yes, she is coming with us. Is that a problem for you?"

"No. No problem. I think she's pretty cool. What is she?"

"Well, right now she's a *doinka* who seems to be infatuated with you." Wheedles chuckled and returned to his cabinet. He pulled out wooden bowls and cups and set them on the table. "Make yourself at home, Joey — this won't take long. You can sleep in the next room, over in the corner you'll find soft bedding. Good night."

"Good night, Wheedles." Joey picked up his camera and went through the doorway to the next room. It was just high enough so he didn't bump his head. "This must be the living room."

Wheedles called from the other room, "They're all living rooms. Everything is living in Waiderfled. The rooms, the grass, the air."

"Oh." Joey wasn't quite sure what Wheedles was talking about, but he didn't want to start another wacky conversation. He just shook his head and looked around the room.

There was an over-stuffed love seat against one wall and a small heavy wooden table in front of it. Two straight-back chairs were on the other side. On the wall across from the entryway was a big fireplace with a black pot hanging inside. Both looked well-used. The bedding was by the fireplace and when Joey walked over to get it, he nearly tripped over the ant-cat.

"Ee-you, ee-you, youuuuuu."

"Oh, sorry ant-kitty. I'll be more careful."

Joey set the camera on the table by the love seat and spread the bedding out in the middle of the room. As he got into bed, he noticed the whole house had a faint smell of dried herbs. It was a pleasant, comforting smell. "Man, this is great!" Joey was on his back and put both hands behind his head. The room was beginning to darken all by itself. He would make sure to have Lou meet him at the culvert for this top-secret discussion, with snacks and would tell him all about Waiderfled, and Lita, and, well — everything!

The ant-cat stepped on Joey's shoulder and then curled up on his chest purring softly as Joey drifted off to sleep. He slept very well that night...

"Rise and greet the day, my friends!" Wheedles called from the doorway and went back to the kitchen. Apparently, it was morning.

For a moment, Joey didn't know where he was. He reached to his chest and found the ant-cat still asleep. He petted her soft fur. "Wake up, girl. It's time to eat."

"Youuuuu," she purred. Then she stretched so hard, all six legs seemed to grow an inch and her corkscrew tail straightened out for a second. She jumped off Joey and trotted into the kitchen. He got up and followed her.

"Good morning, Lita. You look well rested." Wheedles was talking to the ant-cat.

"Lita? She has the same name as that girl who threw me the ho-dree." Joey was in the doorway, rubbing his face.

"There's a good reason for that young man." Wheedles turned to the ant-cat and said, "Lita, show him."

Joey heard the tinkling of bells. He watched Lita curl up on the floor and turn all wavy and see-through. She was shrouded in pink steam (*enough with the pink*, thought Joey) and the next thing he knew, his new pink-haired ant-cat friend was now standing upright in the middle of the kitchen. She was back in focus, looking shyly down at the floor with her hands gently clasped in front of her.

"It is my pleasure to greet you on this fine morning, Joey my friend." She performed the bowing ritual.

Joey's mouth hung open. He was in a momentary daze. She was beautiful. He recovered just enough to return the greeting clumsily. "Uh, yeah, me too." He swallowed hard and his face turned bright red.

"That is a lovely color on you, Joey. How do you do that with your face?" Lita was coming closer, head tilted, and she smiled. He felt her pink and white checkerboard eyes drill holes right through him.

Joey took a quick step back. "Oh, ah, it's just a little magic thing I do sometimes. No big deal." He darted around her and went over to Wheedles. "What's for breakfast, dude?"

"Who's Dude?" Now Wheedles looked at him with a tilted head.

"You. You're Dude."

"What a silly pair you are." Lita stood with her hands on her slim hips. Joey tried hard not to stare.

"The food is on the table. Eat well; we have a two-day journey ahead of us. This will be the last hot meal for a while." Wheedles turned to Lita and spoke to her in their *click-whir-gurgle* language.

Joey sat down at the big table. Although he was picking up more words each time, he didn't pay attention to what they said. While Lita talked to Wheedles, Joey stared. Her shiny pink hair was thick and wavy. It was all the way down to her small waist. She wore a silky pink and blue dress that laced up the front. The skirt was made out of separate pieces of the shiny cloth and the hem of the dress ended in uneven layers just above her knee. Gold threads ran all through the dress. Joey knew that before this whole thing was over, he would *have* to take her picture.

When he realized he was staring at her, Joey quickly looked down at his plate. There he saw what appeared to be thick strips of steaming beef and a mound of something that looked like a cross between curly fries and green beans. "What is this stuff?" The words came out before he could stop them.

They both looked at him like he came from another planet. Okay, for all he knew, he did come from a different planet… dimension… whatever! Wheedles furrowed his bushy blue eyebrows and said, "It's food, Joey — don't you eat where you come from?"

"Oh, sure. Never mind." Joey didn't want to explain that he'd meant *what kind of food.* Wheedles took everything he said so literally. So, he just ate. And whatever the food was, it tasted great.

Everyone finished breakfast and cleaned up. Wheedles packed a few last things and they prepared to leave. There were two large crescent-shaped supply packs. On the way out, Joey picked one up, slipped his camera inside and closed the flap. He slung the strap over his shoulder. Wheedles picked up the other one and grabbed his stick.

As Wheedles closed the door behind them, Joey looked around outside. It was a warm clear morning, and the rainbow sky was wonderful. It was all pastel swirls. He looked over at Wheedles.

"Where are we going, anyway?"

"To the Ho-dree Doctor," Wheedles said.

"Yeah, I know, but where is she?"

"In the Crystal Forest," Lita said. She brushed a few hairs away from her face that were caught by the breeze. Her hair drank in the sunlight and yellow streaks appeared in the thick pink waves. Joey found himself staring, and the more he stared, the more he was terrified that she would catch him staring and he would blush again. Once again, time for distraction mode; he jabbed his finger upward and blurted, "Weird sky, huh?" His companions jumped a little and Wheedles frowned. But no one was looking at *him*, so who cared?

As they walked through the outskirts of town, Joey gradually realized that he could understand everything people were saying. No more *click-whir-gurgle*. In keeping with his new "man of mystery" profile, though, he didn't mention this to his companions. The less he said, the better.

He thought about Lou again, saying to himself *I can'…whoops, I look forward to telling Lou about all of this — he'll go berserk.*

Every now and then, they would pass someone who would stare at Joey and look very disappointed. When that happened, Wheedles would go over, apologize, and explain that Joey did not know the customs of Waiderfled, but that he was a quick learner. They always ended the conversation with the bow and the hand gesture. Joey and Lita would do the same before the three of them went on their way.

When the trio reached the Crystal Forest, Wheedles and Lita didn't hesitate, they walked right in. Joey was speechless trying to take it all in. Open-mouthed and wide-eyed, he stumbled after them. He was trying to look everywhere at once. "This is *amazing!*" Well, at least he'd found something that made him stop staring at Lita.

CHAPTER 8

Quorella Trap

"We've been in the forest for a while now, Joey, and you must have said 'This is *amazing*' a hundred times. Isn't there anything else you can think of to say?" Wheedles had been watching Joey closely for the last fifteen minutes or so.

"It's just that I've never seen - or heard - anything like this before. It's beautiful." The massive crystal trees somehow provided shade, even though they were transparent. They were tinted with assorted colors: gold, brown, green and blue. Joey walked up to a clear brown one and put his hand on the trunk. He could see the veins pulsing inside. The rough bark was warm, and he felt a deep vibration that went through his body. He pulled his hand away.

"It's alive!"

His friends laughed out loud. "Of course, it's alive, Joey," Lita was smiling. "What else could it be? You should be able to tell that from looking at it." Her voice seemed to take on the stringed instrument melody coming from the trees.

"Well, yes of course I can tell they're alive by looking at them, but it's as though they are aware of life, aware of us. They have some kind of energy radiating through the bark like no tree has ever had where I come from."

While shaking his head Wheedles chuckled while he said, "Oh boy, you have more to learn every time I hear you speak, my friend. All of life is aware here, and I bet it is in your world, too. There is only one living force and it takes many forms. You need to really *see* what you look at Joey, wherever you are. Life is always around us."

The ground was covered in noticeably short dark green grass. It was a richer, deeper green than the grass back home, like long moss. It welcomed his feet with each step he took. There were exotic flowers sprinkled everywhere. And there were those small birds with long bodies that buzzed all around, but he couldn't see them clearly. They were too fast to be dragonflies and they seemed to be faster than hummingbirds. They darted through the air in groups, playing a game of tag. "What kind of birds are those?"

"There are many types of birds here — which ones are you talking about?"

"The ones that are all around us."

Lita spoke this time, "Those are not birds, my friend — those are Quorellas."

"Quorellas, huh? Um, that doesn't help me. What's a Quorella?" This language barrier was becoming a little tiring for Joey.

"Quorellas are the creatures of the Crystal Forest. They are very small beings with wings. They live and play here and watch over us. They are shy and usually keep to themselves. But do not taunt them my friend. They can give you a rough time if they have a mind to." Lita was walking next to Joey now. Wheedles was in front of them.

"I'll be sure to keep my distance," Joey said.

"Joey, Wheedles said you still have my ho-dree. May I see it?"

"Sure, did you want it back?" Joey fished around in his pocket and pulled the ho-dree out. Naturally, he was nervous and promptly dropped it. "Oh, sorry." He picked it up and held it out to Lita.

"Oh my, it looks like a stone! I do not want it back my friend… it is my hope for you and now it is yours."

Joey reached in and pulled his own ho-dree out. He put it in his hand next to Lita's. "I really made a mess of these, didn't I?"

He looked at Lita and then over to Wheedles who was using his purple stick as a walking stick and had put a good distance between himself and the two of them. Lita and Wheedles each had four or five ho-drees over their heads. It was odd. He hadn't noticed them today until just now.

"It is not so bad. Mimi-Uno will bring them back. You will see. For now, let us enjoy our journey. We need to catch up to Wheedles. Come on, I'll race you!" Joey heard bells again and saw the cloud around Lita making her go out of focus. Suddenly, she was a little pink bird with white tufts of feathers coming off her head and back. She headed toward Wheedles and was flying circles around him by the time Joey caught up with them.

"So, my friends are getting acquainted. This is good! But we must quicken our pace if we plan to reach the Ho-dree Doctor by tomorrow afternoon."

In the Crystal Forest, walking was no problem — it seemed like the ground helped them along. It was soft and it felt to Joey like they could walk forever without getting tired. They even ate lunch while they walked. It was the same meat Joey enjoyed at breakfast and it tasted even better cold. Every now and then, Lita would fly by and drop off a sprig of berries she'd found somewhere. The berries were the color and size of purple grapes but tasted more like juicy peaches. They quenched his thirst.

They walked until night set in. The crystal trees looked purely magical in the shimmering night. When Wheedles decided it was time to camp, they put down their packs and sat around a small crystal bush. Wheedles slowly waved his purple stick over the bush and chanted,

"Crystal being if you please
light our evening, help us see,
how your presence warms the heart,
until the morn when we depart.
We share our time in gratitude."

While Joey watched this, he heard bells. The bush lit up and Lita joined them in her human form. They ate more of the meat and drank water from the leather flasks that Wheedles had packed for them. After a little conversation and a lot of yawns, the tired trio turned in early.

Joey woke up the next morning to a low, buzzing sound. He didn't even remember going to sleep. Wheedles and Lita were still sleeping. He had used a supply pack for a pillow, and he remembered taking the camera out before he laid down. But that's all he remembered. He must have been a lot more tired than he thought. He looked around for the source of the noise.

There. There it was, he could almost reach and touch her. A girl Quorella, sitting by the foot of a tree looking at him. Her sparkling wings moved back and forth and made the low buzzing noise. She seemed to be trying to figure out what he was. In a single move, Joey slowly reached for his camera and sat up without making a sound. He had to have this picture!

She watched him with curiosity. She tilted her head from one side to the other. The Quorella reminded him of Lita except her hair was light green. His hands were sweating but he kept a firm grip on the camera. He raised it to his eye, caught her in the frame and snapped the picture. The mechanical racket of the old camera spitting out the picture woke his friends.

"By the winds and sea Joey, what have you done?"

"I just took the Quorella's picture. Look she's right over there." Joey pointed to where the Quorella was, but she was gone. "I must have scared her away." The picture hung from the camera like a loose tooth. Joey pulled it out and set it on the ground.

Wheedles and Lita came over and sat down to study the picture. A little color appeared in the middle of the frame.

"By the winds and sea Joey, what magic is this? You took this picture away from the Quorella? If she misses it, she'll come back, and you will be crying in your sleep tonight!" Wheedles was obviously shaken.

"No, Wheedles! When I take a picture, I don't *take* anything from the person, I just make an image of them. It doesn't hurt or anything. It's like a memory of how they looked in your mind except it's on this paper."

As the picture developed, Joey noticed something was wrong. He saw movement inside the frame. It was the Quorella all right, except she hadn't flown away. She was trapped in the picture, and boy, was she mad!

"Geez," Joey whispered. "She's stuck in there. This wasn't supposed to happen." The picture finished developing and the little Quorella was frantically flying back and forth. Every now and then she would stop and bang on the inside of the picture with her tiny fists. She flew back deep into the frame where she became only a little speck. Then she darted back to the front where they saw her up close.

"Oh no! You've captured her and she is madder than a wet mud buggen. Release her — release her now!"

"I *can't* Wheedles."

"What! Joey, how dare you use that word here!" As Wheedles yelled, a tear trickled down Lita's cheek and the Quorella fell to the bottom of the frame, sobbing her little heart out.

"Oh man, I'm so sorry. Please everyone, ca… calm down." Joey's voice caught in his throat. "I didn't mean to use that word, but Wheedles I *am unable* to get her out. This has never happened before."

"You mean to tell me, you bring this magic to Waiderfled, capture a Quorella, and then you don't even know how to release her from that thing? What in all the worlds were you thinking? She'll be so lonely in there."

"I don't know, I just don't know. Please, just calm down and let me think."

Joey could not have felt worse. The trapped Quorella was heart-breaking to look at. But the tears on Lita's face were killing him.

"Please, please stop crying, Lita. I'm so sorry I used that word. I'm so sorry I trapped the Quorella. Just stop crying, I *can't* take it."

"JOEY! Have you lost your mind? You said it again. What is the matter with you?" Wheedles was furious. Joey was horrified.

"Both of you, stop now!" Lita was the only one with any control. "Something has gone wrong here, and we need to work together. It is that simple. In the meantime, we must continue our journey. Wheedles, gather our things. Joey, pick up your Quorella trap and try to comfort her. I do not know if she can understand us. Talk to her with your eyes. She will understand if you focus."

Joey picked up the picture and glanced over at Wheedles. He stood firm with his back to both of them. Lita walked over and looked Wheedles in the eye.

"Wheedles, release this anger at once before it makes a meal of your heart. Focus on your *zwarry* as the Eighteenth King and help Joey rid himself of his enemy within. Do not feed it with your anger." They both turned and looked at Joey.

Wheedles tugged at the bottom of his yellow tunic, and absent-mindedly smoothed it over his bright green pants. "Lita is right Joey, I owe you an apology. This has been a most unpleasant awakening. I lost sight of my *zwarry*."

"What enemy within? What is going on? I'm so confused." Joey looked back at the picture. The Quorella was still sobbing.

CHAPTER 9

The Kidnapped Ho-dree Doctor

The Quorella finally looked up into Joey's eyes. He'd been staring into the picture frame since they started on their way.

"Please little Quorella, I'm sorry. We'll get you out." Joey didn't feel any better. The tear-stained face of this beautiful little creature was all his fault. Her almond-shaped eyes were the same light green as her hair. She blinked with heavy lids but continued looking into his eyes.

Joey concentrated and tried to push his thoughts into the picture as though he was talking to the Quorella. "I'm sorry I trapped you. It was an accident; it wasn't supposed to happen. As soon as I figure out a way, I'll get you out. Can you understand me?"

She nodded. *Lonely, lonely, scared, and lonely,* was what Joey felt from the Quorella. She sat inside the picture, hugging her little knees and rocking back and forth. He thought of the many times his mother had said that he really "captured" that deer in the picture he kept on his dresser. He whispered, "I wonder what she'd say about this shot?" Then, Joey got an idea.

"Hey, Wheedles, can we rest for a minute?"

"Are you tired, Joey?"

"No, I want to try something."

Joey unbuttoned his shirt pocket, took the two-way mirror out and sat down. "I have an idea. She's so lonely in there, maybe she'll feel better if she sees another Quorella."

Lita was confused. "Joey, there are no other Quorellas in sight. They're probably around here somewhere, but they are hiding from us."

"Yeah, but maybe if I put my mirror in front of the picture so she can see herself, she'll think she's not alone."

"What's a mirror?" Wheedles asked.

"This." Joey said as he held it in front of the picture. He tilted it back and forth and then moved it close to the picture. He concentrated his thoughts again, "Look, look over into the mirror."

The Quorella took her eyes off Joey and looked at the mirror. As soon as she saw it, she smiled and motioned to

Joey to bring it closer, closer. Just before he brought it flush to the surface, she stood up. A second later she flew through the mirror and into freedom.

"Whoa!" Joey fell back and laughed. He was so grateful, and he swore he could feel the Quorella's freedom. His voice carried his delight as he called to her, "Yes! You're free little lady."

"Wonderful work, Joey." Wheedles was smiling but Joey could hear the relief in his voice. He pulled Joey to his feet.

"Look out, my friend — she is not through with you yet!" Lita was pointing up.

The Quorella flew straight up, and around in circles until her friends joined her. Then she darted straight toward Joey. She landed on his nose, and his eyes crossed as he tried to see her. Next, he felt the tiniest tickle between his eyes, and a pinch on the bridge of his nose. Then she flew away.

Joey looked over to his friends who looked scared. He rubbed his face.

"What?"

"Oh boy, she got you." Wheedles said seriously.

"What do you mean? She didn't hurt me. I think she tried to pinch me, but it didn't even hurt."

"No, Joey, that's not it." Lita came to him and put her hand on his shoulder; he felt a warm low level electrical current on his skin. "She has arranged for you to experience the Living Nightmare; it is the Quorella way of returning an unkindness."

"The Living Nightmare? What is that?" He was still a bit distracted by her touch.

Lita smiled a little, but her brow was still a bit furrowed, "The next time you sleep you will have a terrible dream and it will somehow be true. It will be linked to something that is happening in your life, usually something that isn't pleasant, and then it becomes an all-encompassing and frightening nightmare. Because Quorellas are wonderful, there will be something there to help you, something of value that you will have to figure out for yourself. But you will be consumed by the imagery and messages of your existing circumstances that are affecting you in your real life. That is why we call it the Living Nightmare."

"Well…okay, if that's all it is, I'll be just fine. I've had lots of nightmares — I mean, they aren't fun, but they're just dreams. Let's get going." Joey wasn't thrilled at the thought of a guaranteed nightmare, but he wasn't about to let Lita know he was scared of a stupid dream.

Lita and Wheedles looked at each other, shrugged, and returned to the trail. As they walked on, Joey started to feel a little better. He slid the empty picture into the supply pack and stared at his two-way mirror for a while before he put it back into his pocket. He was baffled. Joey had no clue as to how the two-way mirror set his accidental captive free, but he was super thankful that it did! And he was seriously stoked that he hadn't taken Lita's picture.

The trio walked on through the morning hours and Joey managed to avoid triggering any further incidents. He thought he could see a Quorella every now and again in the corner of his eye, but he could not be sure. He was slightly more nervous around them now, but the tree melodies, rainbow sky, and odd animal sounds in the forest were soothing. But most of all, he felt a kind of contentment because Lita and Wheedles were treating him like an equal, not an idiot. Some people back home would have really given him a hard time for accidentally trapping the Quorella. He thought about how Lou would have totally urged him to take that picture. At least if he were here, they could both take the blame for the Quorella trap. He kind of wished he had his friend with him now. He was starting to wonder if he'd ever be able to tell Lou about this freakin' world. Then he wondered for the first time if he'd ever see Lou or his home ever again.

"Deep in thought, my friend?" Lita was walking next to him. She smelled like spring, flowers, and the woods. Or maybe it was the Crystal Forest, except the scents grew stronger and more pleasant when she was near.

"Yeah, I guess I am."

"What are you thinking about?"

"Umm, yeah - what great friends you and Wheedles are. I'm glad I can hang around with you guys for a while. I'm really glad Wheedles didn't send me back this morning after I screwed things up so badly. I do that a lot, I guess." Joey felt like some kind of idiot for saying so much. *OMG — why can't I just shut up!?!*

Wheedles came up on Joey's other side. "Send you back now? Oh no, not when there is so much work to do."

"What does your work have to do with me?"

"You are my work. I'm afraid I haven't done a very good job so far. But I will work with you as long as it takes. You see, when I became the 18th King of the Zing Fling, I asked to be transported to that special person who will help me to complete my *zwarry*. When I did that, I was led to you, my friend. Zing Fling Kings travel to all sorts of different lands and when we go there, the worlds are intertwined forever — wherever we go, we strive to forge a friendship that will last a lifetime. Then we will draw knowledge from each other and, as a result, we expand the joy and essence of living to help strengthen the greatness of each of our worlds independently and together. But before we can get started, it is up to me to help you confront your enemy within so you can conquer it once and for all!"

"What enemy within? You guys talked about that this morning. Man, this is all really hard to keep track of. What exactly are you talking about? Are you telling me I'm stuck here for the rest of my life?" Although… that idea wasn't sounding half bad to Joey.

"What I'm saying, Joey, is that you are a special person and someday you will do very special things. Unfortunately, you have given in to the enemy within; it is your personal enemy, who can take complete control and prevent you from achieving your zwarry. That affects a lot more people than just you, my good friend — it affects all of us, those that are near to you, those that you love and those that you will meet in your life."

Joey couldn't help himself; he laughed loud; but when he saw their serious faces, he regained control of himself and asked, "So what are you saying, I'm possessed by an evil spirit or something that's stopping me from making miracles for everyone who knows me?" Just saying those words out loud made Joey burst out laughing again, and his sides were getting a little sore, so he put his hands on his hips, bent over and tried his best to bring it down to a chuckle.

"Well, I guess you could say that." Lita said.

"And what greatness do you think I'm going to do? Cure cancer, stop war, discover a new world? Oops, I guess I have discovered a new world - Waiderfled." He snorted. "Look

Wheedles, you're talking to the wrong guy. Ask George, or my mom — they'll tell you 'Joey means well, but he's got a lot to learn.' My special gift is to mess everything up." This last statement made it easy to stop laughing as he thought about his recent mistakes.

"Who's George?" they both asked.

"He's married to my mom, or *mimi,* I mean."

"Oh, he's your Da-Wonn, or your *dad,* I mean." Wheedles responded proudly.

"No, well, not exactly - he's not my real Dad."

"What? You have fake people where you live?" Lita looked horrified and was covering her mouth.

"No, he's a real person, he's just not my real Dad. My real Dad died right before I was born."

"Oh, so George *would* be your Da-Wonn, if you'd let him. That is your choice I guess." Wheedles said.

"It's not my choice, he and my mom chose each other, and I'm just an add-on to the package."

"Joey, how did your other Dad, your real Dad, die?" Lita asked.

"He worked nights and was killed in an accident on the way to work. My mom told me how excited he was to be having a baby and was looking forward to starting a family. He worked at a glass shop in town and years later, when I asked for a job there, they hired me because they were friends with my mom and they really appreciated all the work my Dad did for them. Anyway, four years ago my mom married George; she really likes him. He adopted me right away, and now he thinks he is my real Dad. He bugs me."

"This is a sad story, indeed. I'm sorry George adopted you." Wheedles furrowed his brow and shook his head, adding "so very sad."

"Adopting isn't bad Wheedles, what do you mean?"

"The way you say it, adopting you means 'bugging you.' I assume that means, makes you feel bad.'"

Joey put his hand up to his forehead and shook his head. "Man Wheedles, I swear I get dizzy talking to you. The fact that George adopted me is actually a very nice thing for him to do. He bugs me because he's always making fun of me; he makes a big deal out of the stupid things I do. He'd still be hassling me about this morning if he were here."

"Why does he do it?" Lita's face was contorted in confusion.

"I don't know… he thinks it's funny, I guess. Anyway, I was thinking earlier how nice it is that you guys don't do that. So, thanks…helps me feel less stupid than I usually do."

"Well, I don't think I care much for this George if he goes around making people feel stupid. That's not good magic. He should make them feel smart if he has that power."

"Wheedles," Joey was exasperated. "I make myself look stupid, George just laughs about it, he doesn't make me that way. Can we talk about something else? Tell me about where we're headed."

"That's a great topic." Wheedles turned to Lita, "Why don't you start us off, Lita?"

"I'd be happy to, Wheedles. We are getting close to the Ho-Dree Hospital which is run by Mimi-Uno, the Chief Ho-dree Officer and her senior staff administrators, Feldmann, and Kalandra, who are both certified Ho-dree Health Officials. All three of them split their time between focusing on the patients and running the hospital. Then there are a number of Specs, or patient specialists."

"Kalandra and Feldmann depend on the Specs; it takes a lot to help the residents heal. I have heard that there is a new patient named Sirma, she comes from the southern lands. As I understand it, she has a particularly tough time managing her ho-drees."

"Joey, you have seen some of the beauty in the ho-drees we all have, but sometimes the ho-drees can become a little dangerous." Lita noticed that Joey was holding the two ho-dree rocks in his hand.

"I guess you have also seen that they can sometimes become very painful. Mimi-Uno works directly with the patients to help them find their paths to recovery. It's different for everyone. Sometimes it can appear to the patients that they are being attacked by their own ho-drees, when in reality, the patients are doing it to themselves. Mimi-Uno helps each of them to find their own path to recovery so they can ultimately control their thoughts and their ho-drees follow. Patients get confused and spend a lot of time trying to control their ho-drees but ho-drees don't have a plan of their own — they just respond to the thoughts of the person. Specifically, the thoughts they have about themselves. Mimi-Uno helps them learn their routines and then Feldman and Kalandra help the patients integrate those routines into their everyday lives."

Joey was struck by the complexity of ho-drees. "That sounds like a super difficult job." Joey immediately became concerned about reintegrating the ho-drees into his life. He immediately thought of all the negative thoughts he had about himself and became concerned that once his ho-drees came back his head would become a ho-dree hamburger!

"It can be Joey," Lita murmured as she strained to see into the distance. The weather seemed more and more beautiful with each passing hour while the forest continued to sparkle and breathe around them. Lita's voice pulled Joey away from his concentration on the forest. "Look there, just over the crest of that hill. It's the Ho-dree Hospital. We're very close now."

The hospital appeared to be at the top of a hill and in front of several lush green hills rolling in the background. Joey's heartbeat and breathing slowed down as he looked at it and wondered what it would be like to live there. It looked spectacular and it seemed so peaceful.

The trio picked up the pace to the Ho-Dree Hospital and a few small out-buildings. As they got closer, Joey noticed the large doors at the front of the hospital and the beautiful flowering bushes and trees surrounding the building. He thought it seemed like a wonderful place to heal. But as they got closer, the vibe was definitely not peaceful. It was just the opposite.

Wheedles obviously wanted to continue the casual conversation they had going, but there was such a ruckus ahead that all three of the travelers began running up to the buildings to see what was going on. Wheedles headed straight over to a tall, skinny man, sporting a green, blue and yellow striped Mohawk hairstyle, who turned out to be Feldmann, the Ho-dree healing official and senior staff member. He had big ears with matching multi-colored hair growing out of his ear lobes. It looked like he was wearing six-inch long, hairy earrings.

"Feldmann! Feldmann! What's going on here?" Wheedles asked as they approached.

"Oh my, Wheedles, by the winds and the sea… so many things! First, it's Mimi-Uno — she's gone. We think she's been kidnapped. And we're trying to get control of our newest patient, Sirma. She is having quite an attack!" Feldmann turned to a chubby lady with cherry-red hair, "Kalandra, please go get Sirma — she's running off into the forest behind the storage shed. Victor went inside to get the headgear. He will meet you there." Kalandra didn't look like she could run very fast, but maybe Victor could, whoever he was.

"Who kidnapped Mimi-Uno?" Lita asked.

"We aren't sure. We don't know why, either. The only one I can think of is Haidderdred; she's certainly evil enough to do something like this. Can you give us a hand with gathering the patients? We've got two patients in addition to Sirma running wild with fright since they found out Mimi-Uno is missing. Victor is a seasoned Spec, but we need more help!"

Joey heard bells again, and Lita turned into the pink bird and flew off.

"Wheedles, use your magic." Joey said.

"My magic doesn't work that way. I have magic over things, not people. I'm afraid we're just going to have to use our heads, our hands and our feet. C'mon, let's help Kalandra!"

Joey and Wheedles met up with Kalandra at the storage shed. Wheedles was in front of Joey heading into the forest when Joey heard whimpering. He turned and saw a girl who had to be the missing Sirma, crouched down behind the shed. She covered her head with her arms to protect herself from the three ho-drees that were whipping around her head.

"Make them stop!" she cried.

"Hey Wheedles, back here!" Joey said, unsure of what to do. He stood there, staring at poor Sirma. The ho-drees bounced off of the shed walls, hit her arms and flew in different directions close to her head. "Ooooo, ouch, that'll leave a mark," Joey muttered as he approached her, ducking to avoid the rebellious ho-drees.

"Ouch, make 'em stop!" cried Sirma.

"Wheedles, come on — she needs help!"

Sirma was sliding further down the wall attempting to lie flat when Kalandra came huffing and puffing around the corner.

"Are you daft, boy? Help the poor girl." Kalandra was angry.

"I don't know what to do!" Joey approached Sirma cautiously. Wheedles ran up to her.

"Here, kid, just catch one." Wheedles stood by Sirma bobbing and weaving like a prizefighter, grabbing at the ho-drees.

"Oh, I get it." Joey ran up and snatched at a green and red ho-dree, but it wouldn't move toward him.

"Silly boy," Kalandra was next to him and caught a blue ho-dree just before it bonked Sirma again. "You can't move it away from her, just stand there and hold it where it is. Don't let go."

As Joey stared at Kalandra, another ho-dree smacked him on the top of his left ear, pinching it against his head.

"Ouch! Wheedles, get that thing will you!"

"Got it."

Joey finally grabbed a hold of the last ho-dree and didn't let go; he held on tight, even though his ear burned, and his head hurt.

"Feldmann, hurry up — we have them!" Kalandra yelled. "Get the head gear from Victor, NOW!" Her cherry-red ponytail flopped around on top of her head as she moved. It was so shiny, it reminded Joey of plastic doll hair. "What are you looking at?"

"Oh, nothing. Sorry, I uh, just, uh... nothing."

"He is daft, isn't he Wheedles?" She was smiling now. "Sirma, it's okay now, we've got them."

Sirma looked up. She was frightened. Her short, white hair was smooth and straight, and her light blue eyes were red-rimmed from crying. She was a small girl, about the same size as Wheedles, with almost transparent white skin wearing a loose-fitting blue shirt and pants that looked like they were made of shimmering silky material. They were exactly the same color as her eyes.

"Who… who… are you?" She looked back and forth from Joey to Wheedles.

"Why, this is Wheedles of Waiderfled, and his daft friend." Kalandra was chuckling.

"I'm Joey Rheelat and I'm not daft." He was irritated with Kalandra but turned his attention to Sirma. "Are you okay, Sirma?"

"Yes, thank you. I'm okay, but I'm so embarrassed. I *can't* control my ho-drees."

At that moment, Joey struggled to maintain his hold on the ho-dree. It seemed to be pulling toward the top of Sirma's head. He held it in place.

"Sirma! Stop it. Do not use that word! You know it makes it worse and you know the rules. Stop undoing your progress. Now say your piece."

"I'm sorry, Kalandra. I'm scared without Mimi-Uno."

"I know you are child, but you are the one that will heal you. Mimi-Uno is just your guide in the healing process, and she's been giving you the tools to manage your ho-drees. Now go on, say your piece."

"I control my ho-drees. I can do anything I choose to do. I am my healing. I control my hopes and dreams. I can do anything I choose to do. I am my healing..." Sirma continued chanting until Feldmann came around the corner.

"Wonderful! Everything is under control back at the hospital and it looks like you have matters under control here. Thanks for your help, Wheedles and..."

"Joey. Joey Rheelat. Wheedles' friend who is not daft." Kalandra winked at Joey.

"Glad to meet you, Joey. Now if you will let me slide in here, I'll get Sirma in the HHG." Feldmann slid between Joey and Kalandra to get closer to Sirma. He held something that looked like a leather helmet with a net on top.

"No Feldmann, you do it. You hold my ho-drees in place, I hate that Ho-dree Head Gear," said Sirma.

Using a gentle tone, Feldman put his hand on Sirma's shoulder and said, "Oh, I know Sirma, but the HHG isn't so bad. I've been holding a lot of ho-drees in place today and I'm a little tired."

"Please, just for a little while? Just a few minutes, until we get up to the hospital? Maybe I can take over then. If not, I'll wear the HHG." Sirma looked so hopeful and so little next to Feldman.

"OK, just until then. But you must help me, Sirma. OK?"

"All right." Joey could hear the relief in her voice.

Feldmann took two steps back and stood with his hands on his hips. He stared at the area just above Sirma's head and squinted his eyes for a moment. "Now get ready everyone."

"Wait, what's going on?" Joey's fear was obvious.

Feldmann continued to squint and said, "As soon as you feel the weight of the ho-dree lighten, open your hand. Everyone ready? Help me now, Sirma."

Joey looked at the ho-dree and felt the weight lift a little. He glanced at Wheedles' hands. They were opening up, so Joey opened his. Kalandra followed suit.

"OK, Sirma, I have them started. Stand up and do your part."

Sirma stared at each of her ho-drees for a few seconds after she stood up. "All right, I'm ready… let go."

The ho-drees hovered around her head just like everyone else's, except Joey's of course; they were in his pocket. Joey kept a close eye on Sirma as they all walked back to the hospital. She was walking so cautiously, with her arms slightly out, like she was balancing on a tight rope. Just as they got to the sidewalk in front of the large, hospital entrance, she started walking more confidently now that she had complete control.

Joey took this opportunity to look around. The grounds were simple compared to the other buildings of Waiderfled. The hospital and the two out-buildings were made from something that reminded Joey of adobe, but they were a deep rich tan color that glistened in the sun. All of them were round on top, resembling giant igloos.

The main hospital lobby was decorated with large potted plants and over-stuffed chairs. It was probably very nice, usually, but everything was such a mess from the patients running wild. There was a lamp in one of the overstuffed chairs and the other one was facing the wrong way. Even the drawings on the wall were all crooked, but it was easy to tell there was a talented artist on site who loved the trees around this area. The two area rugs in the middle of the lobby were pushed aside and folded almost in half. Joey had a hard time decerning the design on them, but it sure was colorful.

The three travelers and the hospital staff broke into clean-up teams after confirming that Sirma could control her ho-drees. Lita changed back into her human self and she and Joey worked on the lobby. Wheedles went back into the hospital wards with Feldmann and Kalandra to clean up in those areas.

Once the debris was taken care of and the furniture was returned to its original position, order was restored, and Joey was able to tour the hospital where he caught a glimpse of some of the patients. One boy was wearing the headgear, officially called the H.H.G. (Ho-dree Head Gear). His ho-drees strained against the net, pulling it down his back.

Every now and again they shot straight up, almost pulling the leather helmet off, and then back down again. In the next room down, Joey saw an old woman asleep in her bed. She had nine ho-drees, all gray and see-through. They were lying down on the pillow just next to her head and they were very still. It seemed to Joey that the lady might be dying or something and it made him kind of sad. He wondered where ho-drees went when their person died, which made him even sadder, so he backed out quietly and figured he should get back to the group and find out what they were doing next.

He followed the sound of talking and found Feldmann mid-tour, "Here are the guest quarters," Feldmann said. "Make yourselves at home. I have to make my rounds."

Joey stood in the doorway, surveying the large round room and saw four more smaller rooms that were attached to this one at the far end through a short hallway. A teardrop-shaped table stood in the middle of the room, with stools made of trees from the Crystal Forest. The stools were sections of logs with the bark still on them. Joey could see into the rich, opaque brown, but not through it. More stools were at the far end of the room and four gold bean bag chairs sat against the wall. All in all, pretty much the coolest rec room he'd ever been in.

"Hey Joey!" Wheedles called out to him, startling him a bit. "We're all going to our rooms to clean up and get ready for dinner. You take the first room on the right down the hall there."

Joey followed Wheedles' suggestion and entered his small but comfortable room. The bed seemed to be a larger version of the bean bag chairs and there was a bathroom to the right of the bed. There was a simple tub/sink and what turned out to be a toilet that looked like a large mushroom with a hole in it and a lever on the wall just above it. "Seems pretty straight forward. Just hope I don't mess up and flush myself into another world." He laughed nervously, because at this point, he was pretty sure that he could make that happen.

One by one, everyone gathered in the rec room. Joey was the last of the travelers to join them. Everyone was chatting and talking about the chaotic day and, of course, they wondered where Mimi-Uno could be and why anyone kidnap her. Joey took Wheedles aside to ask him about the lady he had seen earlier. "I saw an older woman sleeping and all of her ho-drees were grey and just lying on the pillow. Was she dying, Wheedles?"

"Yes, I believe she was, Joey." Wheedles was looking at the ground and seemed very uncomfortable.

Joey asked, "What's wrong, Wheedles?"

"Well Joey, we all understand the end of life comes, it's part of nature. But for that woman, she was never able to achieve and enjoy her hopes and dreams. She fell very ill some years ago and couldn't get out of bed. Now she's in a very deep sleep and will probably not wake before the end."

Joey was sorry he asked, because he felt so bad for her. As Wheedles went back to the group, Joey pulled his ho-drees out of his pocket and studied them for a couple more minutes, resolving to himself that he would do anything he could to fix them. They still scared him a bit, but he whispered to himself, "They're a gift."

Just then, Feldmann appeared. Now that his rounds were complete, he was happy to join them for dinner. It looked like they had a great kitchen staff who brought in all sorts of food for them. There were various kinds of berries, and other fruits along with nuts and something that tasted like chicken but looked like spaghetti. Joey really liked the taste of the clear liquid that seemed to be the only drink. It tasted like lemonade with a dash of cranberry juice.

After the long and tasty dinner, he and his friends settled into the bean bag chairs to exchange stories. Wheedles told the Quorella story, and Feldmann told them how Mimi-Uno was missing when everyone woke up that morning.

"What do you plan to do?" Lita asked Feldmann.

"I have to find her, although I don't know how. There were no clues left behind… she just vanished."

"Maybe she went to visit someone," Joey said.

"No, she would never just pick up and leave. These people depend on her; she always lets me know where she can be reached. There's something wrong and I hope Haidderdred isn't involved." Feldmann didn't explain who — or what — Haidderdred was, but Joey figured he would probably find out soon enough. Whether he wanted to or not.

Wheedles said, "Well, if there were any tracks, they were destroyed by all the running around this morning. Tomorrow, we'll walk around and look for tracks further away from the building area. We'll turn up something." He tried to sound confident, but Joey knew he was worried.

Feldmann turned to Joey, "So what's your story, young man? Where are your ho-drees?"

Joey took his ho-drees out and showed them to Feldmann without saying anything. He was embarrassed.

"Sucked the life right out of them. How did that happen?"

"Well, I guess it's because I used the bad word, and chose not to believe what I saw on my first trip to Waiderfled."

"The *bad word* by itself wouldn't do that, it's what you felt at the time that really did them in. How do you feel now?"

"As dumb as a box of rocks." Joey said, trying to make light of his situation.

"Well, I guess that makes sense now," replied Feldmann.

"Wheedles and Lita said Mimi-Uno could help bring life back into them. That's why we came here."

"She certainly can help bring them back to life, but it's you who will do the healing, young man."

"Me? How?"

"Well, it's not an easy question to answer. Let's just say that feeling 'as dumb as a box of rocks' has left you with a handful of rocks. As soon as we sort things out, maybe I can help guide you. But right now, the best thing we can do is get some rest. Based on your encounter with the Quorella today, I'm confident none of us will get a full night's sleep. Wheedles, you should stay in the same room with him; he'll need a friend before sun-up."

Chapter 10

The Living Nightmare

"Oh yeah, the Living Nightmare. That's okay, Wheedles — I'll be just fine. If I need help, I'll call you." Joey was trying to sound mature, but he was actually feeling a little queasy.

"Whatever you say, Joey. I'll be in the next room." Wheedles stretched as he stood up. "I'm turning in now."

Everyone went to bed. Joey lay awake for quite a while. Now that it was time, the threat of the nightmare was all he could think about. After about thirty minutes, he felt something warm by his ankle.

"Youuuuuuuuuu." It was Lita as the ant-cat, or *doinka*, as Wheedles called her. She snuggled up to his ankle and was making that purring noise again. Before too long, Joey drifted off to sleep.

When he opened his eyes, he didn't see anything. Everything was white — blazing, bright white. He put his hand in front of his face and saw nothing. He turned around and everything was black and empty. He turned in circles: white-black-white-black. He walked toward the white; it was hard to walk, it felt like he was walking through water. After a while, he turned around and walked toward the dark. He was pumping his arms and legs so hard and not getting anywhere; Joey was starting to panic. His heart pounded in his chest and he looked down to see if he could see it beating, but there was nothing there.

"I must be invisible," he said, just before he slammed into a wall.

"Ooofff. Ouch, what's that?" Joey felt for a wall with his invisible hands. It was there, smooth as glass — he couldn't see it, but he sure felt it. There he stood, arms outstretched, leaning on the glass looking into the dark and trying to think of what to do next when suddenly, he saw lights in the distance. He squinted hard and put his forehead against the glass.

The images inside the glass eventually lightened and came into focus. There were six creatures riding horrible-looking beasts and the last three riders carried torches. The beasts were as tall as the front door of Joey's house. Each one had three shiny black horns in a line down the middle of its huge, scaly snout. Dirty fanged teeth jutted out of the bottom of each jaw, curving inward and pointing up to beady, black eyes. Rippling muscles bulged through the dark-greenish black hides. Scaled, serpent-like tails scraped the barren ground as they moved back and forth behind muscle-bound legs that looked like gnarly, old tree trunks. Massive hooves dug into the dirt, sending dust into the air with each brutal step. The ground shook.

The creatures riding them wore heavy clothing, obviously made from the hides of beasts like the ones they were riding. Tight leather helmets covered their faces with holes for their eyes and nose. Scraggly hair stuck out the back of the helmets, making them even more horrid looking.

Joey's attention was drawn to the leader who carried a long spear. His filthy yellow and black hair draped down to his saddle in sticky tangles. A cage, made of wood and bones, was being dragged behind the leader's beast. Inside was a woman with long silver hair and red robes; she was laying on her side. The cage was too small for her, and her slender arms and feet hung out. She was unconscious.

Joey was petrified. He was so scared they might see him that he could hear the blood rushing through his temples. He looked down at his sweaty hands and they weren't there. "Okay right, I'm invisible. They can't see me," he whispered to himself.

Suddenly, the leader let out a piercing screech, turned, and pointed his spear right at Joey. He tried to scream, but no sound came out.

All at once, the whole scene began spinning around, as though the point of the spear was the center of the universe. As it spun faster and faster, the spear point moved closer and closer to him. Joey tried to step back, but somehow the wall was behind him now. The dreadful shrieks of the rider reached his covered ears and Joey's silent screams left him breathless. He was sure he must be suffocating. He shut his eyes, covered his head once more, and turned his back to the attack. After a few seconds, there was silence. He looked over his shoulder and everything behind him was white.

He collapsed into a sitting position, facing the dark wall. Next thing he knew, he was looking into the eyes of the Quorella, except they were the size of basketballs because she was gigantic! Her whole face came into view, and she was beautiful, but huge. Her mouth moved but he couldn't hear her. He pointed to his ears, shook his head and shrugged. He still didn't see his hands, but she was looking him, straight in the eye. Then, her faint voice reached him, and he tilted his head and strained to hear it better. As the voice got louder, he recognized it as Lita's.

"I see you; they saw you; everyone sees you," and the giant Quorella with Lita's voice smiled. "Why don't you see you?" She kept repeating those words. The voice got louder and louder until it started to hurt. Joey covered his ears and shrunk down a little.

"Stop it!" He tried to scream, but it came out as a whisper.

He lay down and rolled over, turning his back to the Quorella. The voice stopped. He lay on his side, still covering his ears, staring off into white. Again, Joey felt like he was suffocating, and his heart pounded so hard, his whole body became the heartbeat. Even his hair moved with the beat.

A face materialized in the white.

"Joey. Joey, help me," she whispered.

He recognized her as the woman from the cage. Her long silver hair was blowing to the side as if there was a strong wind. She had the face of an angel with smooth skin, and silver eyes.

"I see you Joey, help me."

He opened his mouth but no words would come out. Just then, a small dark droplet fell on her cheek.

"Help me, Joey."

A larger drop struck her cheek. It looked like molasses. Then another one…

"Help me, Joey."

CHAPTER 11

Haidderdred

Joey opened his eyes.

"It's all right my friend, you are safe," Lita said, gently resting her hand on his shoulder.

Wheedles stood next to her. "It's morning, Joey — your nightmare came late."

Joey quickly popped his hands in front of his face; he could see them perfectly and they were shaking. "Man, that was horrible. Next time I see a Quorella, you just watch my dust!" Joey shivered. He felt the sweat trickling down his head, his back and his chest. "I need to clean up." He had a bad taste in his mouth.

"Here's a robe, Joey. Victor will take care of your laundry, just leave it outside the door." Feldmann was at the doorway and tossed a red bundle at him. "You'll have to tell us about your Living Nightmare at breakfast."

Joey caught it by the edge and the robe fell open. He gathered it to him and hugged it to his chest. "I really need a shower."

As they left the room, Feldmann asked Wheedles, "Where is his dust? I didn't realize we were supposed to be watching for it. What sort of dust is it?"

"Don't worry Feldmann, this young man utters many words that mean something different than what he is saying. I do not think we were actually supposed to watch his dust. I think he means that he will create a lot of dust the next time he sees a Quorella — perhaps it's a form of camouflage."

When they left, Joey set the robe down and emptied the stuff in his pockets onto the bed: his worldly possessions consisted of one two-way mirror, two messed-up ho-drees, an old Polaroid camera and a couple of lint balls. Feeling slightly under-compensated for all he had been through; he went to the bathroom to clean up. Even after a nice, hot shower, he was still trying to shake the effects of the dream. The long robe was soft and felt good next to his skin. He eventually stopped shaking, but his muscles felt like rubber from being so tense for so long.

Joey joined the others for breakfast, which was fruit and bread. He was ravenous and ate enough for two people.

When he finished he told his companions about the dream. He remembered every single detail perfectly.

"That's it!" Feldmann said when Joey finished. "It was that evil Haidderdred. I knew it!" Feldmann looked over at the jug of the clear juice they were drinking and flicked his head. The jug floated over to him. He grabbed it and refilled his glass.

"How'd you do that?" Joey asked.

"Like I always do," Feldmann answered.

"That's Feldmann's special gift, Joey. It comes in very handy around here with ho-drees flying every which way," Wheedles said through a mouthful of bread and berries.

"We all have different gifts — even you, my friend." Lita dabbed the corner of her mouth with her napkin. "Once you are able to see yourself as you are, you will discover yours."

Feldmann smacked the table with his hand. "Well, enough of all this, we must plan Mimi-Uno's rescue."

"We don't even know where she is," Joey said.

"Of course, we do — your Living Nightmare told us. The woman in your dream is Mimi-Uno, and the people riding the bidder beasts are Haidderdred's soldiers. The dark droplets on Mimi-Unos face are from the Black Blood Caverns, Haidderdred's home. You've confirmed my suspicions, young man."

"Why would Haidderdred take Mimi-Uno?" Lita asked.

"That's still a mystery. It has been two years since we have heard of Haidderdred causing any trouble. She is not as young as she used to be and has lost interest in stealing children's ho-drees."

"Is that why you call her evil?" Joey asked.

"Yes. It is an evil being who steals and eats the hopes and dreams of the children. It leaves them catatonic and sometimes they do not recover. Only the empty shells remain. That's the problem with the old woman you saw in the hospital bed yesterday."

"I thought you said she eats children's ho-drees."

"She was a child when it happened. She is called Izadray and she never responded to treatment; she never came out of it." Feldmann looked down at his lap and shook his head. "We were unable to help her. And now she ages thirty years for every one she lives."

"That's terrible. Why does Haidderdred do it? What does she get out of it?" Joey was disgusted, and feeling even worse about ruining his own precious ho-drees.

"Haidderdred has no ho-drees of her own. It is our ho-drees that keep us young and full of life. She thought that if she ate enough of them, she could create some for herself. She was wrong."

"I've been hit in the head a couple of times with ho-drees and they sure don't seem like something a person could eat. They're hard as rocks."

"Ho-drees of small children are softer. Haidderdred has an evil magic that allows her to pull the essence of the ho-dree away from its owner. Only its gray shell remains. She doesn't eat them the way we eat this food. She absorbs them somehow."

There was a knock on the door and Feldmann got up to answer it. No one was there but Joey's clothes were folded up on the floor.

"Your clothes are ready, young man. We will meet by the storage shed in twenty minutes. Victor will clean up here. He's taken care of our supplies and prepared our transportation." Feldmann handed Joey his clothes and left the room.

"We'd better get going." Wheedles said, though he didn't sound very encouraging.

Twenty minutes later, they were standing around one of those flying contraptions Lita was driving during Joey's first visit to Waiderfled but this one had room for four.

"We're going in that thing - what is it?" Joey asked as he scrutinized the contraption.

It had two wheels, one in front of the other, with a pilot seat above each one. Behind the pilot seats was a double-wide back seat. Small wings flared out from the sides of the machine near the front two seats and three large wings flared out around the back seat area.

"Of course, we're taking this. It's a sky cycle. If we walked, it would take almost two days." Feldmann said.

"On a sky cycle, it will take less than two hours." Wheedles said.

They all climbed in, and the supplies were stuffed in roomy compartments under each of the seats.

"Okay, but where will Mimi-Uno sit when we come back?" Joey asked.

"Wherever she likes, my friend. I can fly, remember?" With that, there was the sound of bells and the pink steam surrounded Lita. A moment later, she was the pink and white bird, flitting and flying around Joey's head. She landed on his shoulder.

"You take the back seat, Joey. Feldmann and I will do all the work."

"Wheedles, where's my camera?"

"Do not concern yourself with that thing. It's safely tucked into one of our bags. I refuse to touch it. I hope you're not planning any more Quorella traps, Oh Great Hunter," Wheedles teased.

"No, the Quorellas are safe. I was thinking more along the lines of a Wheedles trap this time," Joey teased right back.

Everyone chuckled at the banter as they prepared for take-off. The light mood didn't last long, though, as the seriousness of their mission weighed heavily on their minds. Wheedles and Feldmann straddled the wheels and began pumping the sticks. The sky cycle lurched forward. As the pace picked up, the pilots rested their feet on the pegs by the wheels, and the sky cycle took flight. Joey felt the pressure of Lita's little bird feet as she tightened her grip on his shoulder. Her closeness was oddly comforting and somehow gave him a boost of courage in the face of his first flight in a craft that was being kept aloft by a couple of sticks and some pedals.

They flew in a wide circle, climbing higher and higher. Wheedles' blue hair and the hair on Feldmann's ears blew backward with the wind. Joey loved the feel of the wind on his face; it was refreshing and exhilarating. Finally, they cleared the top of the Crystal Forest and headed out over miles of glistening treetops. The swirling rainbow sky was bright, and the day was warm. He could still hear the string melody from the forest and the sun was to his back. Joey wondered if west was still west in this strange world. He moved to the left side of the large seat to look down. As he leaned over the whole sky cycle leaned to the left.

"Center yourself, my friend, or you'll dump us all out."

Lita let go of Joey's shoulder and flew a little distance away. Joey scrambled to the center of the seat.

"Sorry. Didn't mean to rock the boat," Joey called out to his friends.

"What's a boat?" Wheedles asked.

"Never mind," Joey said.

After a while, Joey felt a light weight on his shoulder. He assumed Lita was back when he heard a faint, "I see you."

He looked at his shoulder and his heart skipped a beat. The little green-haired Quorella stood there for a moment, kissed his cheek and flew away.

"Hey Wheedles, can Quorellas talk?" He touched his cheek where she had kissed him.

"Some people say they can, but I don't know for sure. I've never heard one."

"Can they do anything else to you, besides the Living Nightmare?"

"They can bring you good luck with a kiss. But if I were you, my friend, I wouldn't hold my breath." Wheedles chuckled.

"Well, my little green-haired Quorella just left and she said she could see me and kissed me."

Lita landed next to him on the seat and he heard bells again. Both Feldmann and Wheedles turned around at the same time, causing the sky cycle to tip a little, then quickly adjusted for it. Feldmann let go of a stick to brush his long ear hair out of his eyes.

"By the lands and sea, Joey," shouted Wheedles.

"Our journey is a lucky one," added Feldmann.

Joey gave Lita some room as she materialized.

Lita said, "We are lucky to know you." She patted his hand as she spoke and her electrical current moved through him... "Thank you for being our friend, Joey Rheelat." Her dress glistened in the sunlight and her hair drank up the rays again. "You are a special person; this I know for sure."

Joey looked at her, dumbfounded. He tried to think of something to say, but he just kept blinking his eyes and blushing.

"Ahhh, that face magic again. That is a great color for you, I think it's grand!" Her pink and white-checked eyes twinkled as she giggled.

"How long before we get there?" Joey's voice squeaked. He cleared his throat. "I mean it should be soon, right?"

Lita looked out and pointed, "It will be just a little while longer — there's Prism Lake."

Joey looked to where she was pointing. The water sparkled like crystal and as it reflected the rainbow sky, it sent rainbows out to all the bushes and trees making them rainbow colored too, just like a prism does with sunlight. The color gradually turned to earth tones further away from Prism Lake, but there was a river that continued to shimmer and reflect the sky for a great distance until it merged with a vast ocean. The ocean added a deep blue that helped Joey see the horizon.

The colors and reflections and the landscape were more beautiful than anything Joey had ever seen back home. He fixed his gaze on the ocean until it faded out of sight, wishing he could take a picture, but quickly caught himself. Who knows what would have happened? No, he'd leave his camera in the bag for now.

As they traveled on, the trees began to thin out and soon, the land became barren. The beautiful lake and river were replaced with dirt with small patches of brown shrubs and large rocks poked out here and there. Off in the distance, the scruffy patches gave way to small hills that looked like a bunch of bald heads.

"The Black Blood Caverns." Lita said in a low voice that sounded scared.

"We'd better land here and walk the rest of the way," added Feldmann, already beginning the descent.

They circled downward and he landed the sky cycle expertly in the dust. Joey and Lita climbed out and Wheedles and Feldmann jumped off to walk the sky cycle over to a large rock.

"We'll leave it here," Feldmann said. "Help me gather our things."

They each grabbed a supply pack. Joey made sure he had the pack with his camera. They followed Feldmann toward what Joey was sure was their doom in the Black Blood Caverns, the name seemed like an indication. The ground was dry and hard. It felt like concrete under Joey's feet. After walking for about five minutes, they stopped in front of a hill. Feldmann turned around and faced the group.

Using a hushed voice, he said, "We must be very quiet. I don't think there are any soldiers around, but they might be expecting someone to find them, so keep a look-out." Feldmann got down on his hands and knees and climbed the hill. Everyone else followed his lead, trying not to disturb the dust as they crawled. Rocks dug into Joey's palms and knees as he climbed.

Peering over the top of the hill, they saw an entrance at the bottom of the next hill. "We'll go in that way," Feldmann said softly. "Haidderdred uses this side as a back door. There are five or six other entrances around here, but this one is our best option."

The small group laid there for a minute or two, scanning the area for movement of any kind. "Okay, let's go in." A split second before Feldmann stood up, the lead soldier from Joey's dream came out of the heavy wooden door. Everyone ducked behind the crest of the hill.

"I believe that she is searching for trespassers," Wheedles whispered.

"That's a 'she'?" Joey's voice cracked. "She was in my dream. I... I don't think this is such a good idea." Joey tried to sound practical, not alarmed, but it was hard. Because he was petrified.

CHAPTER 12

The Break-in

Over the next few minutes, the band of rescuers took turns scanning the entrance, and it was now Joey's turn to crawl up and peek over the hill to see if the soldier was still there. He was shaking hard now, and the dust clung to his sweating hands, but he valiantly inched his way up until he could see her again. No doubt about it — she was terrifying. Her scraggly black and yellow hair was blowing in the wind and her helmet was pushed up to the top of her head so Joey could see her scarred face. She leaned against the entrance door, chewing on what looked like a big turkey leg. She wiped her mouth with her dirty forearm and picked at her blackened teeth with greasy fingers.

"Oh, gross!" Joey whispered as he slid back down to his friends. "She's disgusting! What a pig!" He wiped his sweaty hands on his pant legs.

"What do you mean `pig'?" Feldmann asked.

"A pig is an animal that eats slop and plays in the mud. Actually, it's just a way to describe a person who looks and eats the way she does."

"Well, I would agree with you then, she is a pig," Wheedles said. "All of Haidderdred's soldiers are pigs if you ask me!"

Joey heard a cackle above his head, "So who's askin' little man?" hissed the soldier.

"It's her!" Lita yelled.

Joey freaked out. His heart thumped, then fluttered, then his whole body was shot through with a jolt of pure adrenaline. "NOOO!" He screamed and jumped straight up to run and -

WHACK!

A sharp pain exploded at the top of his head. He was dazed for a second.

"Wha... what the heck happened?" His friends stood in front of him, with their mouths hanging open. He rubbed his head.

"You knocked her out," said Wheedles. He was grinning. "Excellent work!"

"Interesting strategy," said Feldmann. "Her chin is going to have a nasty bruise when she wakes up. And I expect she will be a little bit angry."

"Are you all, right?" Lita looked into Joey's eyes and knelt down next to him. "I do not think that was a strategy, Feldmann. I believe that was a little bit of Quorella luck."

"Yeah, I'm fine." He was still rubbing his head. "I hope someone else is lucky next time cuz man, it hurts." He felt a lump forming on the top of his head as he got up. "I hope her chin hurts as much as my head when she wakes up. What stinks?"

"She does," Feldmann said as he pointed to the top of the hill with his thumb. "We better drag her over to this side before somebody sees her. We'll tie her up." He dug in his supply pack and fished out a ball of rope. "Remind me to thank Victor when we get back. *If we get back…* thought Joey, his head still throbbing.

Joey and Wheedles topped the hill and each grabbed one of the soldier's repulsive ankles. Her sandals were leather and her feet were black with grime.

"Holy crap! She stinks! What a major-league gross-out!" Joey turned his head as they dragged the disgusting heap over the hill. She smelled like dirty socks, burnt rubber and rotten garbage all at once.

"Roll her onto her stomach. I'll take it from there," said Feldmann.

Lita was holding her nose, "Rebember do gag her bouth."

"What?" Feldmann looked confused.

"Gag her mouth," Joey said, trying not to laugh.

When Feldmann finished, Joey helped him drag the soldier, and her stench, further away, as far down wind as they could get. Then, they regrouped at the top of the hill.

Feldmann rubbed his mohawk and said, "Let's go — quickly! We must get down there before any more of Haidderdred's 'pigs' patrol this area."

They ran on tiptoe in a straight line towards the entrance. Feldmann was in the lead, followed by Wheedles, Lita, and then Joey. He was still pretty freaked out, but at least he couldn't smell that soldier anymore. Feldmann ran straight in the door. Joey and Wheedles followed. Lita stepped aside and Joey heard the bells announcing her shape change as they passed into the darkness.

It was damp and cool in the cavern. The air seemed thick with mildew and Joey heard dripping all around him. Tiny hairs on the back of his neck stood straight up; he had goose bumps. His eyes were still adjusting to the darkness. No one spoke. Feldmann stopped and held something out to Wheedles. Wheedles waved his stick over it and murmured something. A soft blue light appeared between the two of them and Wheedles took whatever it was that Feldmann handed him. Joey jumped when Lita's tiny bird feet gripped his shoulder.

They began walking again. They were forced to lean back a little to keep their balance as they walked down the steep, sloping path. The constant dripping echoed. Joey took short breaths and pressed his hand on his pounding chest, trying to settle his heart.

With the strap of his pouch digging into one shoulder, and Lita's feet digging into the other, Joey couldn't decide which was worse, the discomfort or his anxiety. His stomach was tight and aching; whether it was the result of fear or hunger, he also couldn't decide. Eventually, the path leveled off and the cavern floor became soft and squishy under his feet. It made him think of the skanky soldier's feet, which in turn, made him shiver in disgust. Lita fluttered her wings.

Each time they came to a place where another corridor met the one they were in Feldmann held up his hand and they stopped. He covered his light and carefully checked for soldiers before the group continued. The other corridors were lit with flickering torches; but this hall felt like a main hall and was dark for some reason.

After another fifteen minutes or so of halting progress, Joey heard faint voices in the distance. Just ahead, the edge of Feldmann's blue light was met with the yellow flickering torchlight from another cavern intersection. An evil shriek of laughter drowned out the clanking noises in the distance for a moment. Feldmann stopped and motioned for them to back up. They backtracked a little and huddled around Feldmann's light. Joey saw that the blue light was actually coming from the bundle of twigs Feldmann held in his hand.

"Be very quiet," Feldmann said. Joey strained to hear him. "They are gathered just ahead, in the cavern hall."

"How do you know your way around here, Feldmann?" Joey whispered.

"It's a long story we don't have time for right now. I've been here before, I'm sorry to say."

"What do we do next?" said Wheedles, focused on Feldman.

"Lita, do you think you could fly over and check things out for us?" Feldmann asked, looking at her.

Lita nodded her little bird head and flew off. After a few minutes she returned. The sound of bells seemed a bit too loud as she changed back to her human self.

"There are four of them with Haidderdred. They're eating and Mimi-Uno is locked in a cage. She looks terrible. She's slipping in and out of consciousness. They have her under a stalactite and it's dripping all over her." Lita said, shaking.

"What's that?" Joey asked.

Wheedles whispered, "Stalactites are formed from the dripping minerals. They look like rock icicles clinging to the cavern ceiling and they can form stalagmites on the floor. Look over there." He pointed and Joey saw what he was talking about. "The way I remember the difference is a stalactite holds tight to the ceiling and a stalagmite might form on the floor over time."

Everyone's ho-drees reflected the light, except Joey's of course. He felt foolish in this group because he was scared and had nothing to offer.

Wheedles turned to Lita, "Did you hear their conversation?"

"They were saying `Mimi-Uno will give in. She...well you know, the bad word, she blank last much longer. "

"What is Haidderdred trying to make her give in to?" Feldmann asked.

"I think Haidderdred wants Mimi-Uno to help her with her ho-drees."

"Her ho-drees? Whose ho-drees, Haidderdred's? She never had any before," Feldmann said.

"Well, she has three now. If that's what you want to call them." Lita shivered.

"What do you mean?" Wheedles asked.

"There are three black, droopy things floating around Haidderdred's mangy head. They are dripping with the black blood like the stalactites of these caverns."

"Ughhh, I think I'm going to be sick!" Joey moaned. "Is that what's dripping from the ceiling? Black blood?"

"It's not really blood, Joey," Feldmann explained. "It's water, heavy with minerals that make it look like blood. It's sticky, but after a really long time, it turns hard and smooth when it dries."

"If too much of it drips on Mimi-Uno, she will become encrusted with it and unable to move. She could suffocate." Wheedles said.

"What are we going to do?" asked Joey. He was wracking his brain for a solution. "There must be something!"

Wheedles looked to Lita, "How close together were they sitting?"

"Not very close. Haidderdred is at the head of the table and there are two soldiers on either side."

"Well, here's what I'm thinking: maybe one of us can cause a distraction while the others free Mimi-Uno."

"Oh Wheedles, that will never work," Feldmann said shaking his head. "Haidderdred herself could probably overpower the three of us, let alone the pounding her guards would dish out."

"We're going to need weapons I think," said Lita.

"Wait a minute," Joey said. "What about my camera?"

"Why would they want your camera? Oh …wait," Wheedles was catching on. "You can take their pictures away from them?"

"Yeah, sure, I can totally take their pictures away from them. The further away I am from them, the more of them I can get into the picture. And that way, I don't have to smell them." Joey managed to chuckle even though he was still frightened. "This has got to work!"

"I believe it will if you do, Joey. We must give it a try — it's our only chance since there doesn't seem to be a small army waiting around to help us."

Feldman took charge. "All right. We'll sneak up as close as we can. Joey, you're in front this time. Make your camera ready. Remember, no talking." Feldmann looked as serious as a person with a tri-colored mohawk and hairy ears could look. "Lita, you fly up there again and come right back to let us know if anything has changed. If nothing has changed, see if you can get near Mimi-Uno and let her know we're here."

"Okay, Feldmann," she said. She transformed immediately and hovered around them until Joey got his camera out. "This is crazy. I'm shaking so bad, I'll probably blur the picture." Joey's sweaty hands trembled as he slipped the strap over his wrist. "Can someone take this supply pouch?"

Feldmann held out his trembling hand and Joey gave him the pouch. Everyone was nervous, which somehow made Joey feel a little better. Joey conjured the image from his dream of the desperate Mimi-Uno, and he knew there was no turning back. For once in his life, he was going to do it right, he knew it. He realized it was his responsibility and even though that weighed heavily on him, he found great satisfaction in the idea that for once, he could really help. He stepped in front of the small group and the torchlight cast a tall shadow behind him.

"Come on," he said, "let's get this over with." His mind flooded with the knowledge that they depended on him. He would capture Haidderdred and her soldiers — he had to. He'd taken a million pictures in his life; this was just one more.

He let the words form in his head, "I can do this, I am in control." That reminded him of how Sirma regained control of her ho-drees behind the shed at the hospital. He formed the words he heard her say, "I am in control, I am my healing, I am in control, I am my healing..." Joey let the words roll over and over in his brain. The dream image of Mimi-Uno was still clear in his mind as he led his friends into the flickering torchlight of the corridor.

CHAPTER 13

The Capture

Joey heard the haunting laughter and the clanking of both wood and metal clearly now. He couldn't see the room yet because of the curve in the cavern tunnel.

Feldmann tapped his shoulder; Joey jumped. Then Feldmann pointed around the corner and mouthed out the words "We are here." Joey had figured that out already — by the smell that had hit his nostrils 20 steps back. He stood up straight up and took a deep breath. Then he nodded to his companions.

Joey stepped out to the edge of the wall, crouched down and peeked around the corner. Part of the large room was visible with brightly lit torches lining the walls. The rotting wooden cabinet that was twice his height stood at the opposite end of the room. The animal skins strewn carelessly about the floor were made from the hides of the bidder beasts that Joey saw in his dream. To the left was a large fire pit with a hood over it and pipes that went straight up through the rocky ceiling. The crackling fire roared in the pit and helped cover up the sound of his footsteps. Part of the table where the evil — and putrid-smelling — group was eating dinner was visible, but he could only see a portion of two soldiers' backs.

Joey ducked back around the corner and stood up again. He tightened his grip on the camera and made sure there was still one picture left. He looked into Wheedles' rainbow eyes for a moment and saw, in just that glance, that Wheedles believed in him completely. Joey nodded to him again, took a deep breath, gripped his camera with both hands and sprang into action.

He slipped around the corner as quickly and quietly as he could. Joey was mostly afraid that he was going to wind up sliding in on his butt, but he steadied his footing and focused on the group by the table. As soon as he saw that all five of the hideous soldiers were at the table, Joey tightened his grip on the camera in his hands. Then, just like a bad dream, everything went into slow motion. It felt like moving through molasses as he raised the camera to his eye, feeling the cool rubber of the viewfinder against his skin, and he tried again to steady his shaking hands. Just at that moment, one of them screamed, "Get him!"

Joey caught all five of the thugs in his viewfinder and everything went into fast-forward. All the cups and wooden plates went flying as the soldiers scrambled to their feet. Amidst the chaos, Joey's finger managed to find the button, but a soldier at the corner of the table turned toward him and stood up, partially blocking Joey's view of the head of the table. Joey's heart was pounding so hard he thought he was going to die right there. He heard a chair hit the ground and Wheedles hollered, "Take the picture away now, Joey!!!!" Back to slow motion and in the small space between his hammering heartbeats, he snapped the picture.

While the camera was making its crazy racket to mechanically spit out the picture, Wheedles and Feldmann ran past him into the room. Joey was shaking so hard it felt like convulsions. Still holding his breath, he grabbed the picture from the mouth of the camera and looked over at the empty table. He let the air out of his burning lungs and it came out in a series of painful coughs.

"You did it, my friend!" Wheedles yelled.

"Good going, Joey! Mimi is over there," Feldmann shouted, pointing past the table.

In the far corner, Joey saw a sad sight. Mimi-Uno was still in the cage, under a dripping stalactite, with Lita frantically flitting about over her. Just to the right of the cage, there were four old trunks, recklessly piled up on one another, and next to those was the weapons cache.

There were sheathed swords, spears, battle-axes, bows and arrows and knives. The larger weapons were strapped against the wall and the smaller ones lay on the floor by coils of rope. The room was humid and reeked with the stench that Joey wished he had left behind with the stinky soldier they left outside. Dripping stalactites were in every corner, including the one Mimi-Uno was in.

The others were frantically freeing Mimi-Uno while Joey took everything in. The bell sound Lita made while she changed shapes sounded odd in this dank place, but it helped refocus Joey's overwhelmed mind; he remembered the picture in his hand and examined it. The soldiers were running around in there trying to figure out what happened. There were now three tiny men and a tiny woman. As Joey watched their furious little faces, he felt a sense of pride… until he realized there were only four soldiers in the frame.

"Hey, you guys," Joey yelled, "Haidderdred's not in the picture. Joey ran over to the table. By now Mimi-Uno was out of the cage and sitting on the floor. The three of them were trying to wipe the slime off of her face and arms.

Feldmann turned to face Joey, "You mean you missed her?"

"Yeah, I think so," Joey said as he stooped to look under the table.

"No, Joey. Don't!" Lita cried. But it was too late.

Haidderdred grabbed Joey by the front of the shirt and shoved him backward as she came out from under the table. She had her sword drawn and held it above his head as she pulled him close to her face. Oh, the smell. If she didn't stab him, he might just die of the stench! Something dripped on his face, he glanced up to find out where it came from. It was from one of the greasy, misshapen ho-drees above Haidderdred's head.

Her cold black eyes bored into his, as soulless as a dark infinity.

"Feldmann, if you value the ho-dreeless head of your little friend here, you'll all come over here in front of me where I can watch you."

"Okay, Haidderdred. Take it easy, whatever you say."

Joey heard Feldmann's voice but couldn't turn his head to see if they were moving to where she directed them. He was forced to look at Haidderdred. She was a foot taller than him and bionically strong. Her greasy blonde hair struck Joey as odd. The color of her hair was just normal blonde, very greasy, but normal blonde. Everyone else in Waiderfled had wild — crazy even — hair colors. She was so strong she held him up on his tiptoes with one hand. Her face was weather-worn, and she needed a toothbrush real bad, but she wasn't nearly as ugly as Joey thought she'd be.

"Where are my soldiers, little boy?" she hissed.

"I, I... must have dropped them." Joey no longer had the picture or the camera. "They're safe, they're just in a picture. You made me drop them when you grabbed me."

She frowned and glared at him. He knew she had no idea what he was talking about. She pulled him closer.

"Explain yourself boy!" She actually growled.

"Look over there for a small square." Joey pointed toward the table. "And I'm not a little boy," he added.

She turned her head, saw the picture, and looked back at him. She sneered and then shoved Joey with such force that he careened backwards, arms flailing, trying desperately to catch his balance. It didn't work; he grazed Wheedles and fell on his butt so hard that his teeth slammed together. This made him angry, and he tried to get up, but Feldmann reached over and put pressure on his shoulder to keep him in place. Joey looked at him and Feldmann shook his head. Joey was furious, but he obeyed and just sat there, glaring at Haidderdred.

She walked over and picked up both the picture and camera.

Joey hissed through his teeth in a whisper, "Sorry, you guys."

"All is not lost, young man," Feldmann whispered back. He was looking over at the weapons and jerked his head ever so slightly. One of the spears eased away from the wall, strained against the strap that held it to the wall, and fell back in place. Joey glanced over at Feldmann, and Feldmann winked at him.

Meanwhile, Haidderdred had planted herself next to the table, sword in one hand and camera dangling from her wrist by its strap on the other, like a demented tourist from the underworld. She pinched the corner of the picture trying to figure out what the hell it was. She looked at it, held it out, shook it, and looked into it again. The dangling camera clanged against the sword while all her concentration remained focused on freeing the soldiers from their teeny trap.

Wheedles was sticking close to Mimi-Uno, ready to protect her with his life if necessary. His walking stick was next to them on the ground. Joey watched as Feldmann got Lita's attention and directed it towards the weapons. Using a series of slight eye movements and micro head jerks, Feldmann expertly relayed a message to her. Joey understood that Feldman needed Lita's help to release the strap holding the spears in place. He looked at the weapons again and thought about running over and grabbing a knife.

"By the blood of these caverns little boy, what magic is this?" Haidderdred sounded agitated, but Joey would not even look at her. "Boy! I'm talking to you, you little runt!"

Joey heard movement but he still refused to look at her. He sat there on the floor, with his arms crossed.

"Why, you little..."

Wham! She kicked him in the chest, and he fell back, hitting his head on the cavern floor. Joey saw nothing but blazing white for an instant. He slowly got himself back up to a sitting position, taking just enough time to really feel how angry he was. He was furious, apparently, and in a single, lightning-fast move, stood straight up like a crazed acrobat. His head was throbbing, and his heart was pounding, but he wiped the sweat from his eyes so he could look Haidderdred square in the face.

"Knock it off!" He was now near purple with anger. "Who do you think you are, anyway? Leave us alone."

"Awww, the little boy is getting mad. What are you going to do, big man? You gonna come over here beat me up?"

"I wouldn't touch you with a ten-foot pole, you slime bag! It wasn't you that knocked me over — it was your stench, you pig!"

Haidderdred was laughing now and walked over to him. "Well, it looks like my smell is going to knock you over again you little beast." She dropped the picture and reached over to grab his shirt, but he knocked her hand away.

"Okay, how's this?" she said, and slugged him hard on the chin. After being released from the laws of gravity by her monstrous uppercut, he hit the dirt again and this time, his elbows took the brunt of it and both of his funny bones sent painful buzzing to his hands and shoulders all at once.

"Haidderdred! Stop it!" Feldmann yelled with authority.

Joey was sprawled out on the ground and when the room stopped spinning, "That's enough!" He growled. Joey knew that even if it was the last thing he ever did, he would get his friends out of here and give that low life what was coming to her. Boy, if there was ever a time to pull through, this was it. Just then, Haidderdred appeared over him, dripping disgusting goop all over him. At the exact same moment, Joey heard Lita's bells.

The sound caught Haidderdred's attention, and she looked over her shoulder. As Joey sat up, Lita changed into the bird and flew over to the straps holding the weapons. Haidderdred grabbed for a knife from her belt, while tiny Lita struggled with the strap.

"Oh, no you don't!" Joey quickly rolled over, crashing into Haidderdred's legs to throw her off balance, but she didn't fall.

"You crusty little mud buggen! Get away from me," she screeched at him, and kicked him in the side, knocking the wind out of Joey and leaving him there, struggling to catch his breath.

Haidderdred jumped over Joey and Mimi-Uno, knocking Wheedles out of the way, and headed for Lita. She unsheathed her knife just as the weapons strap fell and Lita flew across the room. Haidderdred threw the knife anyway and it bounced off the wall. She growled, sputtered and cussed while stomping across the room, causing more black grunge to tumble into her eyes.

"These stinking, blasted ho-drees!" In her fury, Haidderdred scratched her cheek trying wipe away the ho-dree grunge.

Out of the corner of his eye, Joey saw a spear floating over to Feldmann. Joey scrambled to his feet in case he could help, but just as the spear got close to Feldmann's outstretched hand, Haidderdred snatched it away.

CHAPTER 14

The Enemy Within

"Feldmann, you idiot. What were you going to do with this?"

"Put you out of your misery, I guess."

Haidderdred held the point of the spear on Feldmann's chest. "So, you would kill your own sister?"

"If necessary," he said softly. "I do not wish to kill anyone. But you have lost your mind, dear sister, and have hurt far too many people."

"Ha!" She backed off a little. "What do you know of pain? Look at your ho-drees, all pretty and bouncy. All of you. Except the little boy here. What's wrong with you, little one? Nothing in your life good enough to hope for? No dreams for your future?"

Joey's anger stung the backs of his eyes. "Oh, I have hopes and dreams for my future." He started walking toward her. She leaned over and grabbed Feldmann by the hair on his ear and pulled him close.

"Hold your ground, boy. Unless you want to see my brother bleed."

Joey stopped in his tracks. Then he heard a soft voice.

"Haidderdred. Stop this. What can we do to help you?" It was Mimi-Uno. She was standing now and using Wheedles' arm for support. "Let us stop this now."

"You know what I want, Mimi-Uno. Fix these blasted ho-drees or take them away."

"I told you. I do not fix these things."

"Well, maybe you'll change your mind after I kill a few of your rescuers."

"I am not saying that I refuse to help. Please listen. You are the only one who can fix them. I can only help guide you to where you want to be. That is how it is done."

Haidderdred shoved Feldmann to the floor and walked over to Mimi-Uno. "Well then, guide me. Do whatever you have to do but do it now." Another drop of gunk fell onto Haidderdred's face. She wiped it off with the back of her arm and then pointed at Joey. "And you, you little runt, get my soldiers out of that thing."

"What's the matter, Haidderdred? You need help taking all of us out?" Wheedles said, taunting her.

"No, I don't. But that's beside the point. My soldiers belong out here with me. Get 'em out now, boy."

"Sorry, no-can-do, lady. They get out when we get out." Joey crossed his arms and looked as defiant as he possibly could.

"Look kid, I'm going to... BLAST THESE HO-DREES!" Haidderdred stopped to wipe the sludge from her face one more time. Mimi-Uno approached her gingerly, took Haidderdred by the arm, and led her to the table.

Joey thought about the situation. Four against one was pretty good odds. But Haidderdred was seriously violent and had an even worse temper than George did. How could it be that she and Feldmann were sister and brother? What a strange land. Joey figured Mimi-Uno felt sorry for Haidderdred in a way. Mimi-Uno looked tired and dirty, but she was still beautiful. Lita hovered on the other side of the room, making herself scarce on top of the moldy cabinet. Joey figured that he had to do something to get them all out of here. It had been his responsibility to capture Haidderdred and her soldiers and he had blown it. He began pacing back and forth. Feldmann and Wheedles were talking and slowly moving closer to the weapons.

"Don't think I don't know what you and your friend are up to, dear brother." Haidderdred jeered. She stood up and flung Mimi-Uno's hand off her arm. "You never cease to amaze me, Feldmann." She picked up her sword, and walked over to Feldmann and Wheedles. "I've been a little sloppy, I guess." She shoved each one down with her free hand, picked up some rope and moved to tie up the two of them.

Joey bolted over to her, still angry. "What are you doing?"

"I can't concentrate with these two hovering over the weapons like this."

"Oh yes you can, dear sister." Feldmann was not exactly thrilled at being tied up. "That's your problem. You believe that you can't do anything."

Joey was shocked to hear Feldmann use that word; in fact, it stopped him in his tracks.

"That's a real good boy. You keep your distance over there. It will only take a fraction of a second for me to cut one of these throats if you start after me again." After she finished tying up the two friends, she pulled a bandana out from under the piles of rope. "Just in case you get any more bright ideas, brother." She blindfolded Feldmann. "You just sit down where you are, boy. I don't think there's any need to tie up a youngster. Now, where were we Mimi-Uno? Oh yes. How long will this take?"

"It might take a very long time. You are going to have to change the way you look at things."

"Well, how long is very long? More than one night?"

"It could take months."

"No. I can't wait months. Fix it now!"

"Haidderdred, you must immediately stop using that word."

"What, you mean 'can't'?"

Mimi-Uno cringed, "Yes. Stop saying it. Stop thinking it."

As the two of them talked, Joey looked around again. He noticed Wheedles was rocking back and forth with his eyes closed softly chanting to the ropes. His stick was a few feet away from him but that didn't seem to be a problem. Lita was behind them, clinging to the back of Feldmann's shirt working on the blindfold. Haidderdred's focus remained directly on Mimi-Uno while she paced back and forth near the table and didn't seem to notice the escape tactics going on behind her.

Joey's thoughts still boiled. A youngster? He was no youngster! He felt stronger somehow. He knew he was going to be the one to end this. He wasn't hoping or dreaming anymore, he knew it, and the decision was made. The very next time Haidderdred was blinded by the dripping black gunk…

"BLAST THESE THINGS!" It happened.

Without a thought for himself, Joey leapt up and tackled the evil Haidderdred. He shouted, "Like I said, I have hopes for my future and everyone else's here!"

He was on her like a rabid dog, and they tumbled down to the floor.

"You little idiot!" Haidderdred's eyes were shut tight from the goop, but she managed to fling him over. He got right back on top of her and was trying to pin her. Of course, she was much stronger than Joey, but he didn't care. "It's over, Haidderdred! I—"

Something was happening. Joey's pocket felt warm, then hot, then it ripped open and the two ho-drees flew out. His silver ho-dree had dark blue lines running through it, but it was his, all right. The pink one was as beautiful as ever and out of nowhere, a bright white one appeared and whacked Haidderdred on the head.

"Ouch, what the heck is going on?" she screeched.

Joey didn't look at the ho-drees long — he had to focus on her. She started rubbing her head where the ho-dree had hit her and he pinned her arms with his knees. He sat up slightly so she wouldn't buck him off.

Feldmann and Wheedles, who were now free, came running over with the rope to tie up Haidderdred.

"I've got you now. It's over." Joey felt a swell of pride and all at once he heard a ZING and a WHOOSH and the white ho-dree grew huge and exploded.

The room was a kaleidoscope. An eruption of colors, sparkles, squiggles, and wind chimes burst out all around them. It was like the first time Wheedles did the Zing Fling into Joey's room, except a million times better. He had never felt anything like it in all his life! Everything was in slow motion, and he noticed that it didn't stink anymore. He looked down at Haidderdred. She looked like she was sleeping, with a ridiculously pleasant smile on her face. Wheedles and Feldmann were laughing and twirling around in the storm of sparkles and squiggles and Mimi-Uno, who was clapping and smiling, bent over and gave Joey an unexpected hug.

Lita's bells joined the wind chimes as she changed into her human self. She danced and laughed with Wheedles and Feldmann. They motioned for Joey to stand up.

Mimi-Uno cried, "You did it, Joey — she is out like a bad ho-dree! You can let her go now. Everything is going to be fine."

Joey was confused, but he was laughing so hard, he didn't care. He tried to stand up and just rolled over. His stomach tickled and he had to rub it. When he spoke, the words tickled his throat, "Wheedles, what's going on?"

"By the winds and sea, Boy, you've just beat your enemy within and realized one of your hopes and dreams at the same time. I do believe you've set a world record as well!"

"Not only that, Joey," Mimi-Uno said, "but you've cleansed Haidderdred of her enemy in the process. It happens like this maybe once in a hundred years, but bless us all, it has happened!"

"See Joey, you are a special someone," Lita added.

Joey looked over at Haidderdred and saw Feldmann fussing over her. "Sister, wake up." He patted her smiling cheek.

"Wha… what happened?" Haidderdred sputtered.

"Joey cleansed you, because that was what you wanted more than anything." Feldmann said.

Mimi-Uno stood over Haidderdred and said, "Mind me now, Haidderdred, a miracle has occurred, and you must keep your mind free of the negative things. Only the positive should enter now or all of Joey's work will be lost on you. We are your friends, your brother loves you, and you are a good person. Remember, you are your healing from now on; you can do whatever you want to do. Say it, Haidderdred."

"I am my healing; I can do whatever I want to do." Haidderdred sat up and looked around smiling while she repeated the words. After a few moments she added, "Whew,

I need a bath," she smacked her lips a few times, "and a toothbrush." Everyone laughed.

"I'm afraid we all need baths," Mimi-Uno said. "Let's pack up and go to Prism Lake. There is reason to celebrate." She held her arms up high and smiled. She looked purely magical in the last of the sparkles and squiggles as they floated to the floor.

The triumphant troop collected themselves and their things and planned their trip to Prism Lake. Lita would fly, Joey, Feldmann, Wheedles, and Mimi-Uno would take the sky cycle and Haidderdred would ride a bidder beast.

"Hey - what about my soldiers?" Haidderdred was holding the picture. "I think they might not like the idea of a bath," she chuckled.

Joey said, "Leave them in the picture, we have one more soldier tied up outside. Maybe you should leave her that way and bring extra bidder beasts. We'll let them all go directly into the water!"

"Good thinking, Joey!" Wheedles said.

Mimi-Uno walked over to Haidderdred and touched her shoulder, "Haidderdred, there is something else. I still have a child patient back at the hospital turning into an old lady. Do you still have the essence of her ho-drees?"

"Yes, I do. I used to sneak back and return them in the night after I found out there wasn't anything I could do with them. Hers are in the cabinet over there; I was so frustrated these past two years; I just kept them. I'm sorry, Mimi-Uno."

"You mean all those children who we thought responded to our treatment were really cured by you?" Feldmann was shocked.

"Yes, dear brother, I'm afraid that's true. I didn't like doing those things, I was just so miserable." Haidderdred walked over to the moldy cabinet and pulled out a clay jar with a lid on it. "Here Mimi-Uno, this is what you need. Do not open it until you are in her room. We don't want to confuse those hopes and dreams of hers. They'll fly directly to her once you get near her."

"Thank you, Haidderdred."

Within an hour, the whole group met over by the stinky soldier, who was wide awake, grunting and snorting and twisting in the dust.

"Phew, what stinks?" Haidderdred asked.

Feldmann just pointed to the stinky soldier and the rest of them laughed.

"Take it easy Rhal, everything's okay. Hey Feldmann and Wheedles, give me a hand." The three of them heaved her up onto a bidder beast. Haidderdred mounted her own beast and waved the picture at them. We'll meet you at Prism Lake, my friends!"

Haidderdred left with three bidder beasts in tow, and Rhal, still snorting and grunting and twisting.

Joey and his friends walked back to the sky cycle and packed their things into the compartments under the seats. In no time they were up and flying with the wind in their hair and Lita flitting about their heads. Joey was thrilled. His stomach still tickled a little and he kept looking up at his ho-drees with a smile that almost hurt. "Man, what a wacky world this is!"

CHAPTER 15

Home Again

It was late afternoon and as soon as they landed, Joey and his friends ran straight into the lake, clothes and all. Lita flew out a little way, and changed into her human self in mid-air and dropped into the water with a splash. She was poetry in flight, as far as Joey was concerned. He finally pulled his gaze away from Lita and went under; the water was cool silk on Joey's skin.

The whole motley crew laughed and hollered and splashed around until they were all squeaky clean. Feldmann got out first and set up a picnic area on the shady hill at the edge of the sand. He had a couple of blankets and the food Victor had packed for them that morning, which now seemed more like three days ago.

"Here comes Haidderdred!" Feldmann yelled. "Welcome, sister!" Everyone came out of the water.

"Hello, brother! Make yourself useful and help me with Rhal — she's as mad as a wet mud buggen."

Rhal's face was red, and she was still grunting and snorting. Haidderdred dismounted and she and her brother dragged Rhal off the bidder beast as gently as they could. Haidderdred took the spit-soaked gag off and Rhal let out a gigantic howl. "Haidderdred, what is going on? What happened to you and who are these rodents? Untie me, and I will cut all their throats!"

"Take it easy Rhal, this is my brother and his friends. Look, I'm free from the black goop and I have a new life. You and I will celebrate by bathing for what I believe to be the first time in your life."

"I'm not taking any blasted bath, Haidderdred. I'd rather die first."

"Well, you just keep saying that. Joey, give my brother and me a hand here, will you?" The three of them dragged the screaming, squirming Rhal into the water and Haidderdred scrubbed her down. After a few minutes of splashing and hollering, Haidderdred pulled Rhal to shore. "Are you going to behave now, Rhal?" Rhal nodded. Both of them were winded. "Okay, I'll untie you and you can finish your bath."

"Okay, Haidderdred. But I still don't like it."

Haidderdred untied her so they both could finish bathing. Haidderdred showed her how to use her finger wrapped with long grass as a toothbrush. That would have to do for now. While Rhal worked on herself, Haidderdred came out of the water. It crossed Joey's mind that she was cute now. Amazing what a little water can do for a person.

"Joey, what about my other soldiers?" Haidderdred went over to the bidder beasts and brought back the picture.

"Oh, I forgot." Joey patted his shirt pocket, and the mirror was still in there. "Dang! I thought I'd lost it." He unbuttoned his pocket and brought out the mirror. "Give me the picture. I'll let them out in the shallow water."

Joey looked at the picture and the soldiers were all sleeping. He jiggled the picture, but they didn't seem to feel it. "Oh well, let's see what happens."

He walked into the water until it was up to his shins. He placed the mirror over the sleeping group and held it face down, above the water. Then he tapped the back of the picture and they fell out at once, knocking him over. Haidderdred was right behind him and picked him up as though he weighed five pounds. "I see you haven't lost any of your strength, Haidderdred."

"I feel stronger than ever, Joey." She turned her attention to the four soldiers. "Okay, everyone is going to clean themselves, or I'll do it for you. Things are going to be a lot different around here from now on."

The soldiers were confused and rolling around, trying to get up and falling all over each other. "Ahhhh, my faithful troops," Haidderdred said with her hands on her hips, shaking her head. "Rhal, come over here and give us a hand, will you?"

Joey joined his friends on the blankets, grabbed a handful of berries and relaxed for the first time in what seemed like weeks. His clothes were already drying out, and a feeling of contentment washed over him.

"So, Wheedles, what now?"

"Well, Boy, it appears I have but one task left today. As the Eighteenth King of the Zing Fling, I will send you home, free of your enemy within."

"You know, all this time I thought you guys meant that there was some kind of spooky spirit or something living inside me. What you were really talking about was what I thought of myself. Right?"

"That is true, my friend," Wheedles said. "The lack of belief in yourself was as real as those bidder beasts over there and twice as ugly. Until you believed that you were the one in control of your future, you would not be free to bring happiness to others. And that appears to be your special gift. As long as you let the enemy within tell you that you were stupid, or useless, or bad, you were not free to see the true you. When you repeat the same negative things to yourself over time, they become your beliefs. You believe they are true from hearing them so often in your head even though they are just made up and definitely not true! It was my job to help you see yourself, how you really are in this life, the real you. No ones' words can make you do or be anything, you must internalize them and keep thinking about them and then finally come to believe that they are true facts — it is what you think about yourself that creates the person you are. So, let's make sure you only think about the amazing you and not the dumb things others may say… use your own knowledge and take care of yourself. We are all learning, every day. If you don't think you measure up in some way Joey, just wait a little while. Choose to learn what you need to learn to become the Joey you want to become."

"With all that said, I had very little to do with the success over your enemy within. We have known all along that you are a special someone. You proved it to yourself, and we all benefited from it."

"Well, I think everyone here is special. You guys have been the best friends a person could ever hope to find. It's a wonderful feeling to have people believe in me, but it's even better to believe in myself. Thanks to all of you."

"We must say so long, Joey, for in your world it is almost morning, and you have a new day to greet."

"Will I see you again?"

"You know you will, my friend, it is our zwarry."

"Maybe it will be under better circumstances next time," Feldmann said.

Mimi-Uno walked up to him, "Joey, we will always treasure this time with you. You have been a blessing to all of us. Remember yourself young man and remember what you have done here." She kissed him on the forehead.

"Thank you, Mimi-Uno."

"Hope to meet with you again, Joey," Haidderdred yelled just before Rhal pushed her into the water.

"So long, Haidderdred and Rhal."

"Take good care of yourself, my friend," Lita said. "Remember I have hopes for you." She kissed him on the cheek, and he, of course, blushed. "Great color on you, my friend." Lita smiled and stepped back.

"I'm not sure what to say to all of you." Joey was feeling sad.

"Say nothing, my friend. We can see you and we know what you feel. Just remember to see yourself, always!" Wheedles raised his purple stick and said,

"Special Joey, a friend you are
and Waiderfled is not so far.
If you need us, simply sing
of the Eighteenth King of the Zing Fling."

"Hey, wait a minute Wheedles — what happened to the other 17 Kings?" WHOOSH - ZINGGGGGGG … and then he heard Wheedles laugh.

"That's a story I'll have to show you another time." Wheedles voice was fading away.

"BYE MY FRIENNNNNDS!" Joey yelled as he traveled up and down, over and over. He floated in colors that were everywhere, inside and out. He twirled and spun and SPLATTT!

Joey hit the waterbed and laid there until the gentle waves stopped. He yawned so wide that his jaw cracked. He was glad to be home. He kicked off his shoes and turned over and went right to sleep.

When Joey woke up, his feet were all wet. He sat up and saw that the cap was off the bed. "Oh no! Mom will kill me." He jumped up, put the cap back on and sopped up the water with the sheets. He threw the sheets and his wet socks into the laundry chute and went to the hall closet to get clean ones.

"Joey, are you up…?" his Mom called from downstairs.

"Yeah, Mom — I'm just changing my sheets."

"You're what —? Good heavens, who are you and what have you done with my son?"

"I'm changing my sheets because the foot of the bed was all wet when I woke up."

"Well, check the cap, maybe you didn't put it on tight enough. You shouldn't have taken it off in the first place."

"Yeah, I know. It's on tight now."

"I swear young man, we're going to get rid of that old thing!"

After he made the bed, Joey sat on the edge, thinking about Waiderfled. Doubt entered his head for a moment, but he said to himself, "No, no way it was a dream - it is real! I know one thing, there's no way I'm letting anyone get rid of my waterbed." He went downstairs to get breakfast.

He was standing at the sink, eating a bowl of cereal, looking out at the woods behind the house when his Mom came in.

"Joey, what happened to your pocket?"

He looked down and saw his torn pocket. "Oh, uh, just rough housing with Lou. Sorry Mom." He was grinning from ear to ear.

"Well, I don't think I can fix it."

"That's ok. I like the way it looks. Don't try, okay?"

"Have it your way Mr. Fashion Conscious." She went back to the living room, shaking her head. When he was sure his Mom was gone, he set the bowl down and said "Yessss! It really did happen! My ho-drees ripped that pocket!" Then he went outside and heard George cussing in the garage.

"Hey, George. What's up?" George had two wrenches in his hands and was working with some pipes on the bench, sort of bashing them back and forth while he tried to turn the wrenches in opposite directions. His next attempt sent one of them twirling across the garage floor.

"Oh, I can't get this dang pipe fitting loose" his voice lowered as he bent and picked up the wrench.

Joey cringed just a little. "Oh, sure you can George, the answer's right there next to you." Joey walked over and took the stuck pipes from George. He put one of them into the vice on the workbench. He made sure it was tightly secured. "There ya go, now just use one wrench — that should break them free."

George looked at Joey with his mouth hanging open. He shook his head a little, set down one wrench and twisted with the other. It broke free. "Well thanks, son," George said, still looking a little shocked. Joey didn't think George realized that he had just said 'son.' But what the heck, it was a new day, so on his way out he said, "No problem, George."

"Let Mom know I'm heading over to Lou's house — we're going on an adventure today."

George chuckled, "Story time in the culvert again?"

"Yep! And I've got a good one!"

The End